Nikki Logan ~~lives on the edge~~ of protected wetlands in W~~estern~~ Australia, with her long-suffering partner and a menagerie of furred, feathered and scaly mates. She studied film and theatre at university, and worked for years in advertising and film distribution before finally settling down in the wildlife industry. Her romance with nature goes way back, and she considers her life charmed, given she works with wildlife by day and writes fiction by night—the perfect way to combine her two loves. Nikki believes that the passion and risk of falling in love are perfectly mirrored in the danger and beauty of wild places. Every romance she writes contains an element of nature, and if readers catch a waft of rich earth or the spray of wild ocean between the pages she knows her job is done.

My Boyfriend and Other Enemies

Nikki Logan

MILLS & BOON

First published in Great Britain 2013
by Mills & Boon, an imprint of Harlequin (UK) Limited.
Harlequin (UK) Limited, Eton House, 18-24 Paradise Road,
Richmond, Surrey TW9 1SR

© Nikki Logan 2013

ISBN: 978 0 263 23514 2

Harlequin (UK) policy is to use papers that are natural, renewable and recyclable products and made from wood grown in sustainable forests. The logging and manufacturing process conform to the legal environmental regulations of the country of origin.

Printed and bound in Great Britain
by CPI Antony Rowe, Chippenham, Wiltshire

Also by Nikki Logan

How to Get Over Your Ex
Once a Rebel…
Slow Dance with the Sheriff
Mr Right at the Wrong Time
Their Miracle Twins
Rapunzel in New York
A Kiss to Seal the Deal
Shipwrecked with Mr Wrong
Friends to Forever
The Soldier's Untamed Heart
Their Newborn Gift
Lights, Camera…Kiss the Boss!

**Did you know these are also available as eBooks?
Visit www.millsandboon.co.uk**

™

To Jo—for your support, your friendship and your unfailingly good judgement over the past ten books.

CHAPTER ONE

TASH SINCLAIR STARED at the handsome, salt-and-pepper-haired man across the bustling coastal café as he exchanged casual conversation with a younger companion seated across from him. The electric blue of Fremantle harbour stretched out behind them. She should have been all eyes for the older man—Nathaniel Moore was the reason she was here, monitoring from across the café like a seasoned stalker—but she caught her focus repeatedly drifting to the modestly dressed man next to him.

Not as chiselled as his older friend, and closer to Tash's thirty than Moore's fifty-odd, but there was something compelling about him. Something that held her attention when she could least afford it.

She forced it back onto the older man where it belonged.

Nathaniel Moore looked relaxed, almost carefree, and, for a moment, Tash reconsidered. She was about to launch a rocket grenade into all that serenity. Was it the right thing to do? It felt right. And she'd promised her mother…kind of.

The younger man reached up to signal the waiter for another round of coffee and his moss-green sweater tightened over serious shoulders. Tash felt the pull, resisted it and forced her eyes to stay on Nathaniel Moore.

It wasn't hard to see what first attracted her mother to the executive thirty years ago. He had a whole Marlon Brando thing going on, and if she couldn't guess it for herself, Tash had dozens of diaries, decades of memories and reflections captured in ink, to spell out the attraction. Adele Porter—she'd abandoned the name Sinclair right after Eric Sinclair had abandoned her—might have had trouble living her feelings, but she had no difficulty at all writing them down in the privacy of her diaries once her divorce had come through.

Tash studied him again. Her mother had died loving this man, and he—from what she could tell from the diaries and family gossip only now coming to light—had loved Adele back.

Yet they'd been apart most of their lives.

She might never have thought to look at those diaries—to look for him—if not for the message she'd received from him on her mother's phone. A fiftieth birthday message for a woman who would never get it made about as much sense as Tash maintaining her mother's exorbitant mobile phone service just so she could ring and hear her voice message when she wanted to. When she needed to.

Because it was *her* voice. And apparently that was what they both needed.

Tash's eyes returned to the man across the café.

Nathaniel's head came up and he swept the diners vaguely with his glance, brushing past her table, past the nameless woman in dark sunglasses disguising her surveillance. That was when she saw it: the bruising beneath his eyes, the dark shadows in his gaze. The same expression Tash had worn for weeks.

Nathaniel Moore was still grieving, and she would bet all of her best art pieces that he was doing it completely alone.

His colleague pushed his chair back and stood, sliding the empty espresso cups to the side for collection by the passing staff. A small kindness that would make someone's job that tiny bit easier. He excused himself to Nathaniel and headed towards the restrooms, crossing within feet of her table. As he passed, his eyes brushed over her in the way that most men's did. Appreciative but almost absent, as though he were checking out produce. A way that told her she'd never be going home to meet his family. That said she might get to wear his lingerie at Christmas but never his ring.

The story of her life. Ordinarily she would steadfastly ignore such a lazy appraisal, but today…the chance to see what colour his eyes were was too good to resist. She turned her head up fractionally as he passed and crashed headlong into his regard. Her breath caught.

How had she, even for a moment, thought he was the lesser of the two men? Not classically handsome but his lips were even and set, his jaw artistically angled. And those eyes… bottomless and as blue as the rarest of the priceless cobalt glass she'd worked with…. They transformed his face. Literally breathtaking.

She ripped her stare away, chest heaving.

He kept walking as if nothing had happened.

Her heart tugged against her ribs like a nagging child and she took a deep, slow breath. She wasn't used to noticing men beyond their mannerisms, their social tells, the things that told her who they really were. With him, she'd been so busy studying the shape of his mouth and the extraordinary colour of his irises she'd failed to notice anything else. She'd failed to think of anything else.

Like the reason she was here.

Her focus dragged back to the water's edge and the man sitting there alone, staring out.

Do it.

The voice came immediately. Not her mother's and not her own. A weird kind of hybrid of both. But it was the reason she was here today and the reason she'd paid particular attention to a newspaper article in which Nathaniel Moore was captioned in the photograph. The reason she was able to find out where he worked and, then, how to contact him. The voice that was just…planting seeds. Inspiring particular actions. Pushing when she needed a nudge. Kind of like a guardian angel with an agenda, prompting from off-stage.

Do it now.

Tash's hand reached for the call button on her mobile even as her eyes stayed glued on the greying man across the alfresco area. He reached into his suit pocket casually, tugging his tie a little looser, winding down a notch further. She was about to dash all of that against the rocks of the harbour side they sat on. Tash very nearly pressed the 'end' button but he flipped his phone open as she watched.

'Nathaniel Moore.' Deep and soft.

Tash's heart squeezed so hard she couldn't speak and a frown formed between elegant eyebrows.

He lowered the phone to check the caller ID. 'Hello?'

Speak! Her mouth opened but the tiny sound she uttered was lost in the café noises. He shook his head and started to close his phone. That was the shove she needed.

'Mr Moore!'

He paused and lifted his eyebrows, speaking again into the phone. 'Yes?'

She took a deep breath. 'Mr Moore, I'm sorry to interrupt your lunch—' *Damn!* She wasn't supposed to know where he was. But he seemed to miss the significance. She narrowed her eyes and looked closer. In fact, he seemed to have paled just slightly. His hand tightened noticeably around the phone.

'Mr Moore, my name is Natasha Sinclair. I believe you knew my mother.'

Nothing.

Tash watched expressions come and go in his face like the changing facets of good glass. Horror. Disbelief. Grief. Hope.

Mostly grief.

His free hand trembled as he fidgeted with a napkin. He didn't speak for an age. Tash watched his panicked glance in the direction of his lunch partner and she twisted slightly away as his gaze dragged back past her table.

Eventually he spoke, half whispering, 'You sound just like her.'

It sickened her to be doing this to a man her mother had loved. 'I know. I'm sorry. Are you all right?'

He reached for the water pitcher and poured a glass. She heard him take a sip even as she watched him raise a wobbly glass to his lips. 'I'm…yes. I'm fine. Just shocked. Surprised,' he added, as though realising he'd been rude.

Tash laughed. 'Shocked, I think.' She took a breath. 'I wanted to call you, to touch base. To make sure you knew…' Yes, he already did know; his expression spoke volumes.

Silence fell as Nathaniel Moore collected his emotions. He glanced towards the restrooms again. 'I did hear. I'm sorry I couldn't come to the funeral. It was…not possible.'

Tash knew all about the fall-out between their two families; she'd seen the after-effects repeatedly in her mother's diaries. 'You didn't get to say goodbye.'

He looked desperately around the café and then turned his face away, out to the harbour. His voice grew thick. 'Natasha. I'm so sorry for your loss. She was…an amazing woman.'

Tash took a deep breath and smelled a heavenly mix of spices and earth. She knew, without looking, who was passing her table again. Broad, moss-green shoulders walked away from her towards Nathaniel Moore. He spared a momentary, peripheral glance for her. It was the least casual look she'd ever intercepted.

Her heart hammered and not just because her time was running out.

'Mr Moore,' she urged into the phone, 'I wanted you to know that regardless of how your family and mine feel about each other, my door is always open to you. If you want to talk or ask any questions…'

The younger man reached his seat, recognising immediately from the expression on the older man's face that something was up. Nathaniel Moore stood abruptly.

'Uh…one moment, please…will you excuse me?'

Was that for her or for his colleague?

Nathaniel moved unsteadily from the table, indicating the phone call with the wave of a hand. Concerned blue eyes followed him and then looked around the café suspiciously. Tash threw her head back and mimed a laugh into her mobile phone as the stare sliced past her. Not that he'd have a clue who was on the other end of Nathaniel's call but she absolutely didn't want to make difficulties for the man her mother had died loving.

Not for the first time since finding the diaries, Tash imagined how it would feel to be loved—to love—to the depths described in such heart-breaking detail on the handwritten pages. Her eyes drifted back to the younger man now sitting alone at the waterside table.

'Are you there?'

'I'm sorry, yes.' She found Nathaniel where he stood, back to her, half concealed in giant potted palms. She groaned. 'Mr Moore, I just wanted you to know that…my mother never stopped loving you.' The Armani shoulders slumped. 'I'm sorry to speak so plainly but I feel like we don't have time. Her diaries are full of you. Her memories of you. Particularly at…the end.'

Her heart thumped out the silence. His posture slumped further.

'You've lost so much.' His voice was choked. 'Endured so much.'

She glanced back to the table. Hard blue eyes watched Nathaniel from across the café, narrowing further.

Tash shook her head. 'No, Mr Moore, I *had* so much.' *More than you ever did. More than just one extraordinary night together.* She sucked in a breath. 'As hard as it has been to lose her, at least I had her for my whole life. Thirty years. She was a gift.'

The greying head across the alfresco area bowed and he whispered down the phone. 'She was that.'

Silence fell and Tash knew he was struggling to hold it together. 'You should go. I've called at a bad time.'

'No!' He cleared his throat and then glanced back towards his table, sighing. Blue-eyes stared back at him with open speculation. The hairs on Tash's neck prickled. 'Yes, I'm sorry. This isn't a good time. I'm here with my son—'

Tash's focus snapped back to the younger man. *This* was Aiden Moore? Entrepreneurial young gun, scourge of the social scene? Suddenly her physical response to his presence seemed tawdry, extremely *un*-special, given that half the town's socialites had apparently shared it.

'I have your number in my phone now.' Nathaniel drew back to him the threads of the trademark composure she'd read about in business magazines. 'May I call you back later, when I'm free to speak?'

She barely heard the last moments of the call, although she knew she was agreeing. Her eyes stayed locked on the younger Moore, realisation thumping her hard and low. He couldn't be compelling. He couldn't smell as tantalising as an Arabian souk. She couldn't drown in those blue, blue eyes.

Not if he was Nathaniel Moore's son.

The Moores hated the Porters; and the Sinclairs, by association. Everyone knew it, apparently. Why should the heir be any different?

It took Tash a moment to realise two things. First, she'd let down her guard and let her eyes linger on him for too long.

Second, his ice-blue gaze was now locked on her, open and speculative.

She gathered up her handcrafted purse, slid some money onto the table and fled on wobbly legs, keeping her phone glued to her ear as though she were still on it even after Nathaniel had returned to the table.

She felt the bite of Aiden Moore's stare until she stumbled out into the Fremantle sunshine.

CHAPTER TWO

THE WOMAN IN front of him was barely recognisable from the one he'd seen in the café, but Aiden Moore had learned a long time ago not to judge a book by its cover. She may have looked fragile enough to shatter last time, but watching her wield the lance with the molten ball of glass glowing on its tip, watching the control with which she twisted it and lifted it closer into the burning furnace, and he was suddenly having doubts about the likelihood of her caving to a bit of his trademark ruthlessness. That strong spine flashing in and out of the light coming off the blazing magma ball didn't look as though it lacked fortitude.

His plan changed on the spot.

This woman wouldn't respond to one of his calculated corporate stares. She wouldn't sell out or be chased off. Waiting her out might not work either. The focused way she persuaded the smelted glass into the shape she wanted with turn-after-agonising-turn of the rod spoke of a patience he knew he didn't have. And a determination he hadn't expected her to.

She lifted the glowing mass—whatever the hell it was going to be when finished—and balanced the long tool on an old fashioned vice, then reached forward with something resembling tin-snips and started picking away at the edges of the eye-burning mass of barely solid glass.

She was tiny. She'd peeled down her working overalls in

the heat and tied the arms around her waist, leaving just a
Lara Croft vest top to protect her against anything that might
splash or flare up at her from her dangerous craft. Incredibly confident or incredibly stupid. Given how hard she'd
worked to catch his father's attention, he had to assume the
former. He'd bet his latest bonus that her eyes would hold an
intelligence as keen as the rapidly cooling shards she sliced
away from her design—if they weren't disguised behind in-
dustrial-strength welding goggles. In the café, it had been
oversized sunglasses. She'd used them well to disguise her
surveillance, but he'd finally twigged to how much attention
the stranger across the restaurant was paying to his father.
And how hard she was working to hide it. The moment she
realised her game was up she took off, but not before he got
a good look at the line of her face, the shape of her lips, the
elfin shag of her short hair. Enough to memorise. Enough to
recognise a week later when she turned up in the park across
from MooreCo's headquarters.

And met his father there.

She plunged the entire burning arrangement into a nearby
bucket of water and promptly disappeared in a belching surge
of steam. It finally dissipated and Aiden realised that her
body was still oriented towards her open kiln, but her face
had turned to where he stood in the doorway, those infuriating goggles giving her the advantage. Tiny droplets of steam
clung to every one of the light hairs on her body, making her
look as if she were made from the same stuff she was forging.

But this woman was a mile from fragile glass.

'Mr Moore. What can I do for you?'

It took him a moment to recover from the brazen way she
immediately admitted to knowing who he was. She didn't
even bother faking innocence. More than that, the soft,
strained lilt of her voice; nervous but hiding it well. He found
it hard not to give her points for both.

How to play this? *'You can end your affair with my father,'* was hardly going to effect change. Except maybe to set those tanned shoulders back even further.

He cleared his throat. 'I was hoping to purchase a few pieces for our lobby. Something unique. Something natural. Got anything like that?'

She could hardly say no, he knew; everything she had was like that. He'd taken the trouble to search the web before coming here. Tash Sinclair had quite the reputation in art circles.

She pushed the enormous tinted goggles up into pale, sweat-damp hair. 'That's not why you're here.'

Aiden sucked in a slow, silent breath. The goggles left red pressure marks around the sockets of her eyes but all he could look at were the enormous chocolate-brown gems shining back at him, as glorious as any of her glass pieces. And full of suspicion.

Immediately, a ridiculous thought slipped into his mind. That they had each other's eyes. He had his mother's dark, European colouring and her blue, blue eyes. Whereas Tash Sinclair was practically Nordic but with brown eyes that belonged in his face. The combination was captivating.

'It may not be why I came, specifically, but I do mean it. Your work is amazing.' He wandered permission-less into her studio and examined the pieces lining the shelves. An array of tall, intricate vases; turtles and manatees and leafy seadragons, extraordinary jellyfish detailed in fine glass. This wasn't where she displayed her works but it was where they were born. The genesis of her expensive pieces.

Only her eyes followed as he moved around her space. In his periphery, he saw her lift trembling fingers to her messy hair, then curl them quickly and shove them out of sight behind her back. His eyes narrowed. Despite working on his father, she could still find time to be concerned about whether she looked okay for him.

Charming.

But it gave him an idea. If Little Miss Artisan here was hell-bent on hooking up with his father, perhaps the most effective weapon in his arsenal wasn't from his corporate collection of steely glares. Or his chequebook. Perhaps it was something more personal.

Him.

If she was after the Moore name or Moore money, he had both. Maybe she'd allow herself to be diverted from his father—his married-thirty-years father—in favour of the younger, single model. Long enough for him to do some good.

If she cared what he thought when he looked at her, then he had something to work with.

Mind you, if she knew what he *really* thought when he looked at her she'd probably run a mile. She might work with fire every day but she didn't look as if she regularly played with it. Not the way he had. He liked it rough and he liked it short and blazing with volatile, brilliant, ambitious women. About as far from a tiny, tomboyish artsy type with big, make-up-less eyes as you could possibly get.

Which would make it all the easier to remember not to blur the lines. He was the toreador and she was the bull. His goal was to keep her eyes on him long enough that she'd forget her obsession with his father. To keep dancing around her in big flamboyant circles drawing her farther and farther from the family he was so desperately trying to protect.

His mother had sacrificed her life raising him. The least he could do was repay the favour and help keep her husband faithful.

If it wasn't too late.

'Make yourself at home,' she mocked, one eyebrow raised, stripping off protective wrist covers and tossing them on her workbench.

He swallowed a smile and glanced at the still-steaming bucket. 'What are you working on?'

'It was a practice piece for an ornamental vase. I wasn't happy with it.' She pulled the rod and the inadequate creation on the end out of the nearly evaporated water. The glass had completely shattered. She nodded to a series of coloured glass sticks laid side by side on the workbench. 'Those will be lorikeets mounted around its mouth.'

'I'll take it.'

'It's not for sale until I'm happy with it.' She laughed as she tossed the waste glass into a recycling bin off to one side. The two sounds melded perfectly. 'Besides, you don't strike me as someone who would appreciate a pink lorikeet vase.'

'I appreciate quality. In all its forms.' He lifted his eyes intentionally and locked onto hers. Classic Moore move.

Doubt-lines appeared between her brows, drawing them down into a fine V. But where he'd expected a blush, she only looked irritated. 'If you still like it when it's done, I'll make you a pair for your reception desk. At a price.'

'I'm not expecting mates' rates.'

'That's good, because we're not mates. I don't even know you.' Her dark eyes shone. 'But you know me, it seems. What really brought you here?'

Aiden used silence to best advantage in boardrooms. The speed with which an opponent rushed in to fill a thick silence said a lot about them. But the one he unleashed now ticked on for tens of seconds and the diminutive woman before him simply blinked slowly and waited him out, serenity a shimmering halo around her.

Well, damn...

He broke his own rule. 'You were watching us at the café.'

Those eyes widened just a hint. She took a careful breath, shrugged. 'Two good-looking men...I'm sure I wasn't the only one looking.'

The blank way she said it made it feel like the opposite of a compliment. 'You met my father last week.'

She took a careful breath. 'Across the street from your offices. Hardly clandestine. Does your father know he's being monitored?'

'I was passing by.' *Liar!*

'Does he know I'm being monitored, then?'

Aiden blinked. The woman was wasted in an art studio. Why wasn't she working her way rapidly up one of Moore-Co's subsidiaries? For the first time he got a nervous inkling that his father's interest in the pretty blonde might not just be connected to those full lips and innocent eyes. Natasha Sinclair had a brain and wasn't afraid to use it.

'Have dinner with me.'

Her instant laugh was insulting. 'No.'

'Then teach me to blow glass.'

The shocked look on her face told him he'd just asked her for something intensely personal. 'Absolutely not.'

'Make some custom pieces for MooreCo.' That was work; she was a professional artist. She couldn't refuse.

He hoped.

Those dark eyes calculated. 'Would I be required to go to your offices?'

It was a risk, putting her so close to his father, but he'd be there to run interference. Moreover, it would allow him to keep her close; where all enemies belonged. Win her over. And gather more information on what this thing between her and his father was all about. 'For consultation, design and installation.'

She wavered. His own brilliance amazed him, sometimes.

Her eyes narrowed. 'Will you be there?'

Oh, that was just plain unkind. 'Naturally. I'm the commissioning partner.'

If a *humph* could be feminine, hers was. 'When do you want me there?'

He mentally scanned through the appointments he knew his father had, and picked the most non-negotiable one. One taking his father halfway across the city. He named the date and time.

Nothing wrong with stacking the deck in his favour. It was what he did for a living. Find opportunities—make them—and turn them into advantage.

She reached up for her goggles. 'Okay. I'll see you then.' Without waiting for his answer, she re-screened her soul from his view, pressed her steel-caps onto a pedal on the floor and turned towards a brace-mounted blowtorch that burst into blue-flamed life.

Aiden let his surprise show since she was no longer looking. He'd never been so effectively dismissed from his own conversation. Firm yet not definably rude. Had he even had control of their discussion for a moment or was that just a desperate illusion?

Still, at least he'd walked away with what he'd set out for, albeit via a circuitous route. Whatever Natasha Sinclair and his father had going on was thoroughly outed. And he was now firmly wedged in between any opportunity for her to engage with his father.

Couldn't have worked out better, really.

If not for his already monumental ego, Tash would have kissed Aiden Moore.

He'd handed her the perfect excuse, the other day, to get closer to her mother's lost love with his transparent commission. She'd been hit on enough times to know the signs. And the likely outcome. Every guy she'd ever dated had started out by buying something of hers. Or expressing interest in it. She'd lost interest in those kinds of sales—those kinds of men—no matter how lucrative.

She knew from firsthand experience that men with Aiden Moore's charisma and social standing didn't plan lifetimes with women like her. Women like her made terrific mistresses or fascinating show-and-tell at boring dinners or boosted your standing in local government in an arts district.

She'd met—and dated—them all.

Not that she cared. Aiden was a Moore and she was a Porter-by-proxy and if he hadn't already joined the dots he soon would and that would be that. Their families' feud would only add to the antagonism he so clearly felt towards her.

Because that had to be what was zinging around the room when he was in it.

Nathaniel had told her to put their family differences out of her mind. But it was easy to be dismissive of a family feud when you were the cause of it. She had simply inherited it. So had Aiden.

She jogged up the railway-station steps into daylight and wandered towards the Terrace, her trusty sketchpad under her arm. The excitement of a new commission bubbled away just beneath the surface, hand in hand with some anxiety about seeing Nathaniel again. So publicly. He'd changed an important meeting when he'd heard she was coming in, embracing the opportunity to get to meet her in a work capacity. To legitimise all the sneaking around they'd been doing.

She was sure they both considered it worth it. They spent hours chatting about her mother, about their families, their lives. Nathaniel Moore wasn't a man to regret his choices but he was human enough to need to set some ghosts to rest. And she was motherless enough to want to hang onto Adele Porter-Sinclair no matter how vicariously.

'Natasha. Welcome.'

The silken tones drifted towards her from the kerbside taxi

in front of the MooreCo building just as she approached it. Aiden leaned in to pay the driver, then turned and escorted her into his building with a gentle hand at her back. She ignored it steadfastly.

The first time she'd been here, she'd been too nervous to appreciate her surroundings. Now the enormity of this opportunity struck her. MooreCo's lobby was high, modern and downright celestial with the amount of West Australian light streaming in the glass frontages. Tiny dust particles danced like sea-monkeys in the light-beams. The best possible setting for glasswork.

'You'll just need to sign in.' Aiden directed her to the security desk.

Once she was done, the security guard slipped her an ID tag and smiled. 'Thank you, Ms Sinclair. I'll let Mr Moore know you're on your way up.'

The deep voice beside her chuckled. 'He knows.'

'I'm sorry, Mr Moore, I meant the senior Mr Moore. He's waiting for Ms Sinclair's arrival.'

The masculine body to her left stiffened noticeably. Couldn't be helped. Nathaniel was an adult and could socialise with whomever he chose. Whether his son liked it or not.

Aiden's jaw clamped tight. 'Up we go, then.'

The elevator ride was blessedly short and horribly tense. Aiden's dark brows remained low even as he stole sideways glimpses of her in the mirrored wall panels. Tash did her best to remain bright and carefree even though she was sure it was infuriating him further. The elevator climbed and climbed in silence and, just as Aiden opened his mouth to speak, it lurched to a stop and a happy *ding* ricocheted around the small space.

Saved by the bell. Literally.

The elegant doors parted and Tash all but fell out, eager to be moving again. A familiar face waited at the landing.

She stepped forward and extended her cheek for Nathaniel's waiting lips.

'Natasha. Such a delight to have you here. An unexpected delight.' He directed a look to his stony-faced son. 'I was not aware that the two of you knew each other.'

'I might say the same, Father.'

He ignored that. 'I believe you are to create some wonders for our entry lobby, Natasha? I look forward to seeing the designs.'

'I look forward to working with you—' common courtesy demanded she say it '—both. Shall we get started?'

They turned down a long hall. 'Your meeting with Larhills?' Aiden murmured towards his father.

'Conveniently delayed.'

'Ah.'

Tash saw the older man slip his hand onto his son's shoulder. 'A change of fortune. I wouldn't have appreciated missing Natasha's visit.'

Aiden held the boardroom door respectfully. 'How do you know each other?'

'I knew her mother.'

I loved her mother. Tash heard the meaning behind the words ringing as clear as the elevator bell. Even Aiden narrowed his gaze as he followed them into the generously appointed boardroom overlooking the wide blue river to the leafy riverside suburb beyond it.

'But I didn't know of her stunning artistic talents until very recently,' Nathaniel went on. 'Let's see what she can do for our shabby foyer, eh?'

She could practically smell Aiden's frustration and confusion, and a small part of her pitied him. If not for the predatory way he'd tracked her down and tried to ask her out. If not for the likelihood that he'd toss her out on the street when he found out she was a Porter in disguise. Commission or no commission.

But the anxious furrow that he hid from his father wheedled its way into her subconscious and brought an echoing one to her brow, and she felt, for the first time, guilt for barging into their perfectly harmonious lives with her bag of secrets.

She placed her hands serenely on the polished jarrah table. Timber was too clunky and dense to have ever interested her much but she recognised the craftsman and knew his price tag. Just a pity she wasn't planning to charge Nathaniel for this commission. No, this would be a gift from her mother to the man she'd loved.

'Your foyer light is perfect for glasswork,' she opened, speaking to Nathaniel. 'Well oriented for winter light and high enough for something cascading. Something substantial.'

Aiden's left brow peaked. 'We've gone from a pair of vases to "something substantial" very quickly.'

She turned her eyes to him. 'The space determines the piece.'

'I would have thought I'd determine the piece,' he pointed out, 'being the commissioner.'

She flicked her chin up. 'Commissioners always think that.'

Nathaniel laughed. 'It may be your commission, Aiden, and your creative offspring, Natasha, but it's my building. So it seems we're equal stakeholders.'

She turned her head back to him, quite liking the idea of being partners in something with Nathaniel Moore. Even if it also meant tolerating his son. 'You own the whole building?'

She hadn't realised quite how wealthy the Moores were. Entire buildings in the heart of the central business district didn't come cheap.

'Did your price just go up?' Aiden asked.

'Aiden—' Disapproving brown eyes snapped his way.

'I'm interested because that means you don't need to get the buy-in of the other tenants. That will save a lot of time and hassle.'

Nathaniel nodded. Satisfied and even pleased with her answer. 'So, shall we talk design?'

In Tash's experience, the number of times a man glanced at his watch during a business meeting was directly proportional to how important he believed he was. A man like Aiden should have been flicking his eyes down to his wrist on the minute.

But he never did. Or if he did, she never caught him at it. He gave her one hundred and ten per cent of his attention.

Nathaniel was similarly absorbed and entirely uncaring about the passing of time, it seemed. But at the back of her mind, she knew what ninety minutes of a company's two top personnel must be worth.

'I think I have enough to get started with,' she said. 'I can email you some early designs next week.'

'Bring them in,' Nathaniel volunteered and Aiden's eyes narrowed. 'We can have lunch next time. It's a bit late to have it now.'

Not if you asked her gurgling stomach. She'd been too nervous to eat beforehand. Still, there were more than a dozen cafés between here and the railway station. Hopefully, their kitchens would still be open. 'Okay. That sounds lovely.'

Aiden frowned again. If he kept that up, he was going to mar that spectacular forehead perpetually.

Their goodbyes were brief; she could hardly give Nathaniel the open-armed hug she wanted to in an office full of eyes— even if his all-seeing son weren't standing right there—and so she left him standing as she'd found him, on the landing to MooreCo's floor. Aiden summoned the elevator for her and then held the door as it opened. As if to make sure she actually got in it. When she did, he stepped in as well.

'You must have somewhere better to be,' she hinted. Somewhere other than stalking her.

'I'll call you a cab,' he murmured.

'I'm taking the train.'

He stayed on her heels as she stepped out into the foyer. 'I'll walk you to the station.'

'I'm stopping for something to eat.'

'Great. I'm starving.'

She slid her glance sideways at him. *Subtle.* Most men at least feigned some reason to hang around her long enough to hit her up. Aiden Moore didn't even bother with excuses. She slammed the brakes on his galloping moves.

'I'm not going to go out with you, Aiden.'

He turned. 'I don't recall offering.'

'No. You just assumed. Our relationship is professional.'

Speaking of excuses…

His pale eyes narrowed. 'It's just lunch, Natasha. I'm hardly going to proposition you over a toasted sandwich.'

She straightened her shoulders. 'In my experience that's exactly how it goes.'

The assumption. The entitlement.

His head tipped. Something flickered across his expression. 'Then you've had the wrong experiences.'

She laughed. 'Hard to disagree.'

She spent the last four years of high school disappointing the raging hormones of boys who thought her hippy clothing reflected her values. Being disappointed by them in turn. Waiting for the one that was different. The one who liked her for who she was, not for what they thought she might do for them. To them.

And then, after graduation, the men who wanted an unconventional arty sort on their trophy wall. And then Kyle…

'Lunch. That's it.' He peered down on her, a twist to his lips. 'Until you tell me otherwise.'

Ugh. Such a delicate line between confidence and conceit. One she couldn't help being drawn to, the other sent her running. She'd had her fill of supercilious men. She fired him her most withering stare and turned for the exit. In the polished glass of the building's front, she saw the reflection of his smile. Easy. Genuine.

And her gut twisted just a hint.

Nice smile for a schmuck.

They stopped outside a café called Reveille two blocks down, probably better for breakfast but beggars couldn't be choosers. Aiden chose a table at the back.

'So how do my father and your mother know each other?'

The question took her aback. She'd not expected him to ask outright.

'Did.' She cleared her throat. 'She died last year.'

He frowned. 'I'm sorry. I didn't realise.'

'No reason you should.'

'How did they originally know each other?'

'They went to the same university.'

True. And yet not complete. The whole truth wasn't something she could share if he hadn't already done the maths. It wasn't her place.

'That means your mother and mine may have known each other, too. That's where my parents met. Although she dropped out before graduating so perhaps not.'

Tash held her breath and grabbed the subject change. 'She didn't finish?'

He smiled at the waiter who brought their coffees. 'My fault, I'm afraid. Universities weren't quite so family friendly back then. My grandparents pulled her out of school when she got pregnant.'

'She never went back? Finished?'

'I think child-rearing and being the wife of an up-and-coming executive rather took over her life.' His eyes dimmed. 'She sacrificed a lot for me.'

'You're her son.'

'I'm still grateful.'

She didn't want to give him points for being a decent human being. Or respond to his openness. She wanted to keep on loathing him as a handsome narcissist. 'Do you tell her that?'

He glanced up at her and she found herself drawn to the innate curiosity in his bottomless eyes. Opening up in a way she normally wouldn't have risked. 'The first thing I regretted when I lost Mum was not telling her all the obvious things. Not thanking her.'

For life. For opportunity. For all the love. Every day.

His eyes softened. 'She knows.'

Was he talking about his mother or hers? Either way, it was hard not to believe all that solid confidence. He didn't understand. How could he? Plus, Aiden Moore's business was none of hers, and vice versa.

She handed him a menu. 'So were you serious about a toasted—?'

'Are you a natural blonde?' he asked at the same time. The menu froze in her fingers. But he hurried on, as if realising how badly she was about to take that question. 'It's your eyes…I thought blonde hair and brown eyes was genetically impossible. Like all ginger cats being male.'

Her frost eased just a little and she finished delivering the menu to his side of the table.

His eyes grazed over the part of her visible above the table before settling back on hers. 'Unless they're contacts?'

'I've had both since birth. And I've met a female ginger cat, too. It happens.'

Kyle's old ginge was a female. One of the things that let her get so close to him was how loving he was of that cat. Turned out how people treated animals *wasn't* automatically a sign of how they'd treat people. Just another relationship myth.

Like the one about love being unconditional.

Or equal.

She opened the menu and studied the columns.

Aiden took his cue from Natasha, but he knew what was on the menu and he didn't really care what he had. The meeting before theirs had been a luncheon so he wasn't hungry. At least not for food.

Information he was greedy for.

Her mother was dead. That explained why the woman wasn't hovering on the scene discouraging her daughter from dating a man twice her age. Maybe it explained the vulnerability in her gaze, too. But one personal fact wasn't nearly enough.

He'd work his way slowly to what he really wanted to know.

'Have you been a glass-blower all your life?'

She didn't look old enough to have had time to become a master at her craft. With her sunglasses holding her shaggy hair back from her lightly made-up face, she looked early twenties. Fresh. Almost innocent.

But looks could be deceiving. She was old enough to have a reputation for excellence in art circles and old enough to have worked out that there were faster ways to make money than selling vases when you looked as good as she did.

'Twelve years. We went to a glassworks when I was in school and I grew fascinated. I started as a hobby then took it up professionally when I left school.'

'No tertiary study?'

Her chin came up. 'Nothing formal. I was too busy getting my studio up and running.'

'It's a good space,' he hinted. 'Arts grants must be pretty decent these days.'

Her lips thinned. 'I wouldn't know. I haven't had one for years.'

He studied her closely. 'You're fully self-sustainable just on your sales?'

'I traded pieces for studio space until I was established enough to sell commercially.'

'So somewhere there's a crazy Tash Sinclair collector with a house full of glass seahorses?'

She shrugged. 'He had empty commercial space and I had investment potential. Our boats rose together.'

'Ah, a patron.' Of course.

Her eyes darkened for a heartbeat, then flicked away. 'At the time. Now he's the mayor.'

Kyle Jardine. He knew the man. Big fish, small pond. Always a little bit too pleased with himself given what little he'd actually achieved in life—mid-level public office. Exactly the sort of man to be suckered by a hot, intriguing gold-digger.

'A *notable* patron.'

Her lips twisted. 'Notable enough to drop his support the moment he had candidacy.'

Ironic that an opportunist should find herself so treated. And now she was working up his father to fill the vacancy for sucker?

She flicked back her hair. 'Except him cutting me free made me discover that I could stand on my own. So, yes, I've been self-sufficient for two years now. I own my studio thanks to him, I own my house, thanks to Mum, and I make my rates and put something better than fast-boil noodles on the table at night thanks to my seven-day-a-week glass habit.'

'And thanks to your reputation. Your pieces don't come cheap.'

She shifted in her seat but held his eyes. 'As you're about to find out.'

He chuckled and then asked something off-script. Something just because he was curious. 'It doesn't bother you that Jardine got rich on your talent? Then cut you loose?'

She looked as if she wanted to say a whole lot more on the subject but thought better of it. 'He can only sell them once. I can make a new one every week. Besides—' she smiled at the woman who came to take her order '—when you're an artist, every single piece you sell is going to make someone else more money than it made you. Nature of the beast. It doesn't pay to get attached.'

Did that go for people as well? Was that a survival tactic in her world?

She turned to order. All-day breakfast. Totally unapologetic that it was nearly four o'clock. He ordered something small and a second coffee. This was going to be an interesting meal.

'So why the fascination with nature?' All those sea creatures and birds and stormy colours.

She considered him and then shrugged. 'I make what the glass tells me to. Usually it's something natural.'

'"The glass made me do it." Really? That's not a bit... hippy?'

She smiled. 'I am a hippy. Unashamedly so.'

If she was, she'd reined it in today. Dark crop top with an ornate bodice over the top, and a full skirt. Feminine and flowing. He couldn't see her feet but he itched to know whether she'd have sandals or painted nails or—something deep inside him twisted sharply—a toe ring. Maybe tiny little bells on her ankle. Some ink?

Get a grip, Moore. Fantasising about a woman's foot decoration. Pervert.

'What?' she asked, a breadstick halfway to her mouth.

He composed his expression. What had he betrayed? He scrabbled his way to something credible. 'I have a memory,' he said. 'Of my parents. When I was young. My mother was dressed a bit like you. I think they might have been a bit… organic…in their day.'

She smiled. 'What was that, mid-eighties? The New Age movement would have been burgeoning about then. It's very possible. Or did you think your father was born in a business suit?'

The memory that his subconscious spat up when he needed the lie became manifest. He *did* remember his mother dressed loose, earthy and free. Down by a river somewhere. Laughing with his father, her arms wrapped around Aiden as a toddler. The memory even had that Technicolor tinge, the way old photos from the eighties did.

But, it was his mother's happiness that struck him as incongruous. It had been a long time since he'd had any memories at all where she'd looked at his father like that. Adoring. Engaged.

Maybe it was more figment of imagination than of memory.

Because he kind of *had* thought his father was born in a suit. And some days it felt as if he had been, too. Mergers and acquisitions did that to you after a decade or two. He couldn't imagine father or son on their back in the grass by a river. Picking shapes out of the clouds. Breathing in synch with the tumbling water.

The water feature out front of MooreCo was about as close as they got. And the last time he was on his back in the grass…?

Not a thought for a public place.

'So you don't know a lot about your parents' past, then?' she asked, her face carefully neutral. As if he wouldn't notice her poor attempts to elicit information about his father. Maybe information she could use in her seduction.

He fixed his jaw. 'Before I came on the scene? No, not really. I know they met at uni. He was doing a double-major in commerce and law and she studied arts until she withdrew at the end of second-year.' All pretty much public record. 'That's about it.'

'Aren't you curious?'

'Not especially. It's ancient history.' If they'd had any friends at university, they didn't stay in touch into adulthood. If they had, he'd have known. They'd be amongst the endless honorary aunts and uncles that visited the Moore home when he was younger.

Which made it strange that Tash's mother didn't rank amongst them, now that he thought about it.

Almost as strange as realising he now thought of her as Tash.

She lifted one brow. 'Or is it more that it doesn't involve you so it doesn't rate?'

Ouch. Had he been that much of a jerk since meeting her?

Yeah, probably.

'My family are close but they've always tried to keep the kids out of the old business.' In fact, in his family the kids got knuckle-rapped for sticking their noses into anything adult.

Which was how he knew exactly how pissed his father was going to be when he realised his son was running interference with a gold-digger. But he didn't care. He was hardly going to stand around and let Natasha Sinclair lure his father's attention away from his wife of thirty years like some toe-ring-wearing siren.

His father was a handsome, rich man. Ambitious women came and went regularly. But generally they didn't make a ripple. In all the years they'd worked together, he'd never seen his father so fixated on a woman. Especially such a young woman. Though he knew there'd been at least one time…. It was infamous in his family and no one talked about it above a whisper.

So, like it or not, he was going to keep himself right up in their faces and on alert. If she wanted to mess with a wealthy Moore, she could have a crack at the heir. He was more than capable of taking her on, and—as his body tingled at the thought—more than willing.

Maybe some of her free spirit would rub off on him like a breath of fresh air.

He didn't know.

Or, if he did, he had an outstanding poker face.

Nothing about that had changed in the week since she'd first sat in this boardroom.

Tash glanced out at the suburbs across the river stretching off beyond the horizon. The MooreCo building executive floor had to have one of the best views in town.

Aiden Moore seemed entirely oblivious to their parents' shared past. Exactly as oblivious as she was before she'd opened that first diary. For a whispered-about family secret, this one was surprisingly well maintained. She was hardly in a position to enlighten him.

She glanced at both men. *By the way, did you know that my mother and your father were lovers?*

She didn't owe Aiden any loyalty just because they were offspring-in-the-dark in common. Her loyalty lay with Nathaniel—her mother's love—and outing them both to Aiden would damage more than just his relationship with his own father. They were close, she could see. Not close enough to share secrets—and she had no doubts that Aiden had his fair share, too—but they were respectful of each other where it counted and disrespectful enough to speak of a close, affectionate relationship. Much closer than she could ever imagine with her own father. Their humour was pretty much aligned with hers and she had to concentrate on not smiling as they gently ribbed each other.

She wasn't part of this family, even if she felt like it.

She was an outsider.

All this affection and father-son camaraderie wasn't for her to enjoy. No matter how she craved it. And no matter how connected she felt to them. How much she felt as if—inexplicably—she belonged here with them.

'All right,' she said, sitting forward. 'So everyone's happy with the design?'

Six little scale models in glass and a large pencil sketch decorated the table between them. Fish of various sizes, seahorses, a diving kestrel, strips of kelp, a sparkling school of krill. 'And this will be the shards of sunlight cutting down through the ocean.'

Nathaniel smiled, but he wasn't looking where her fingers pointed. 'We've never had anything like it in any of our buildings. It will be astonishing.'

'How much is it going to cost?' Aiden asked, lips pressed.

So the arctic thaw over lunch the week before was only a lull, it seemed. Just as she might have relaxed.

'Aiden,' his father barked. 'Unimportant.'

Tash moved to ease the sudden tension between the two men. 'This is a showpiece for me. I'll be doing it for material costs only.'

Aiden frowned.

Nathaniel sat up. 'No, Tash. You mustn't…'

She locked eyes on his. 'I'm not going to charge you, Nathaniel. Not for my time. But there'll be a lot of glass in this piece so if you'd cover that I'd be grateful.'

Insisting would just be awkward and she'd handed him a chivalrous out. But, of course, this was Nathaniel. 'Naturally we'll pay for materials but…' He pursed his lips and

thought for a moment. 'What we really need is a public an-
nouncement. That way you get the PR benefit in lieu of payment for your time.'

'I don't require payment for my time.'

Aiden's eyes darted between the two of them.

'Well, I wish to show off this marvellous design and if I
choose to do that in front of my corporate equivalents and that
just happens to lead to more work for you, so much the better.'

'Nathaniel—'

'It's decided. I won't protest at you not charging MooreCo
for what I'm sure will be a considerable amount of your time
and artistic focus, and in return I expect you to be gracious
and professional about my desire to throw a party to celebrate
the acquisition of our biggest ever art piece.'

Snookered.

She glared at him. Then very *un*graciously snorted. 'Fine.'

His smile was immediate. 'Good girl.'

Aiden's left eye narrowed.

She met his gaze and held it.

'That's worked out well, hasn't it?' he asked flatly.

But she got the sense that he really wanted to add '...*for
you*' to that.

CHAPTER THREE

TASH STEPPED OUT of the expensive vehicle onto the highest heels she owned. Their engineering had always seemed pointless, but she'd take the extra inches against Aiden any day.

'I'm still struggling to understand why I needed to be *invited* to a party in my own honour?' she said.

'Think of it as more of a VIP escort than an invitation,' he murmured.

Uh-huh. She would have believed that from his father, but not from Aiden. Although it was entertaining to imagine him as an escort. Upper-case E. He was slick, handsome and full of fakery enough for it...and he had the right body.

'Something amusing?'

Tash forced her lips into a more serious line. 'No. Just appreciating the architecture. I've never been inside this building.' The second part was true, at least.

'You're in for a treat. It's beautifully restored.' His hand dropped to her lower back as he guided her up the stairs and through the ornate doors. Heat from his fingertips tingled through the soft fabric of her dress. 'I thought you would have seen the glasswork, at least. That's why we chose this as a venue for the launch party. And this time of day.'

She let her eyes drift up to the stunning stained-glass windows on the western side of the building practically glowing in the rich, low afternoon light. 'I've seen them from the outside, of course.'

'Natasha. Aiden.' Nathaniel moved towards them, as dapper and handsome as ever. 'Did you arrive at the same time?'

Aiden's chin lifted the tiniest bit but it was enough to put paid to his lie about her needing an escort. But it was too entertaining watching him trip up on his own transparency to make a big deal of it. She leaned in for a kiss on each cheek from Nathaniel then glanced around the beautifully appointed venue. Up on the big screen her glass prototypes had been photographed and lit by a professional and looked about as good as the finished artwork would. The AV team flicked quickly through them in rehearsal for the speeches later.

'This is all so beautiful. Are all your parties this lavish?'

'Usually. Aiden sets a high bar.'

She turned her surprise to him. 'This is your work?'

'I didn't personally choose the flowers, if that's what you're asking, but I do know the quality planners in town and how to get the best out of them.'

I'll bet.

'Will you forgive me?' Nathaniel said. 'The inexcusably prompt are starting to arrive.'

He waved his arm in a flourish and the visuals on the big screen ended with a snap as the lights sank in a subtle cross-fade with the music that grew out of the silence around them.

And just like that, it was a party.

Aiden's hand was back at her lower spine again but where before it had only tingled, now it blazed with un-ignorable heat. Either he'd developed a raging temperature in the last thirty seconds or hers had inexplicably plunged. So much so that tiny bumps prickled up all over her back.

'Would you like a drink?' he murmured, close to her ear.

How galling. That his charm and charisma should have actually had some effect. She spun away from his gentle touch.

'You don't actually *need* to escort me, Aiden. I'm quite capable of getting safely to the bar.' Or not, since she didn't drink much and certainly not at work events. 'I'm sure you'll have better things to do this evening than shadow me.'

And as the word slipped unconsciously across her lips she realised that was exactly what he was doing. Babysitting her. Controlling her arrival and departure and her movements while here.

Why?

'Tonight is very important to my father,' he simply said. 'I'm on hand to run interference should anything go...wrong.'

Interference? By sticking close to her? 'What is it you imagine I'm going to do here? Lie back on the bar and drink shots straight from the bottle?'

His blue eyes crackled. 'I would pay good money to see that.'

'I'm sure you would, given some of the other things you're famous for spending your money on—' she ignored his flare of surprise '—but I've been to many of these nights, Aiden. I know the drill. Turn up, look good and be wild enough to be interesting but not inappropriate. Intrigue but don't offend. Generate speculation but not gossip.'

It was all about appearances. And buzz.

She fronted the bar and ordered a virgin cocktail in a fast and low breath. If he noticed the virgin part, he didn't comment. The important thing was that it *looked* like something harder. But she'd be in full control of her faculties all night.

He frowned. 'Is that what you think you're here for? Entertainment?'

She turned and drew a long sip of her drink through the pretty glass straw. A clever and thoughtful touch given the focus of this evening. 'This is a little different, I'll admit. But the principle doesn't change just because the date does.' Not that he was her date... 'The important thing is that I won't be doing anything to embarrass Nathaniel in front of his associates.'

'You think I'm worried about that?'

'I don't know what to think, Aiden. All I know is you've been playing me since the day we met and running *interference*—' it felt so good to throw his own word back at him '—between myself and your father. MooreCo has already given me a massive commission. What more do you imagine I'm trying to screw him out of?'

His dark brow lifted. 'Your word, not mine.'

Realisation rushed in, tumbling and tripping over astonishment. How stupid she'd been not to see it before. The straw dropped from her gaping lips. 'You think I'm *hitting* on your father?'

For the first time, he dropped the casual veneer and that carefully neutral expression simmered with something else entirely. Something quite captivating in its passion. 'He's obsessed with you. And you shower him with your attention and your come-hither smiles and keep him dangling, helplessly, in your thrall.'

Come-hither? She wasn't sure what offended her more: the suggestion that she was consciously trying to seduce Nathaniel or the realisation that any interest that Aiden had shown in her until now was purely strategic. 'He's a grown man, Aiden. I'm sure he's managed to fend off women much more beautiful and much more skilled than I am in his fifty-five years on the planet.'

'Then why the interest?' he urged. 'Why him?'

Her chest tightened. 'He knew my mother.'

Aiden snorted and tugged her around behind a large potted arrangement, out of view of the arriving guests. 'Then go hang your neediness on one of her other friends. Leave my family out of it.'

Her breath backed up in her gridlocked chest. The term

needy cut her much deeper than it should have but something bigger than that stole focus. A clue about what this was all really about—and who this man really was.

'Family? I thought we were talking about money.'

His nostrils flared wildly. 'Because it's always about money with you?'

It was almost *never* about money with her. Even with Kyle she'd believed he had genuine feelings for her. Money was just what brought them together. That and necessity. 'I think that's just what you expect. Because it's the language you speak.'

He snorted. 'You're trying to tell me money doesn't talk.'

'It talks; I'm a realist. But it's not what makes the world turn.'

She might as well have sprouted antennae; he looked at her as if she were from another planet. 'Please don't say love,' he sneered.

'I was going to say people. People are what matter, but, yes, love is part of that. For each other. For our *families.*' She leaned on the word extra-hard.

'You'd rather be loved than wealthy?' Disbelief dripped from his handsome lips.

'You say that as if it's worse than preferring to be wealthy than loved.'

'Maybe it is.'

She stared at him. 'Is your mother like this?'

Instant granite. Eyes, face, body. 'What does my mother have to do with anything?' he gritted.

'You are so unlike your father, attitudinally. I can only assume it's your mother's influence that has made you like this.'

'Like what? *Un*like you? If you are so damned hippy about love and people and flowers and sunshine, I'd have expected you to be more accepting of the differences between us.'

That would have niggled less if not for the peace-symbol

tattooed on her ankle. 'I'm not *un*accepting of the differences. I'm just trying to understand them.'

'Why? You don't like me. You don't want to be around me. What the hell does it matter?'

Was it possible that he was wounded by her lack of interest in him—way down deep where the bluff and bluster didn't penetrate? She stared into those hard eyes and found it impossible to believe.

'I guess it doesn't matter.' Though that didn't stop her from being interested...*way down deep* where her protective veneer didn't penetrate. 'Except that you've made stalking me your personal project so I get the feeling we'll be seeing a lot of each other.'

His laugh was short. 'If I'm stalking you I'm doing a lousy job.'

'No. Not stalking. Your brand of creepiness is much more overt.'

The moments the words were out, she regretted them. Not that anything he'd said to her these past minutes was particularly polite but branding a man *creepy* was quite an indictment. Especially when he was commissioning your next work.

He reeled for just a moment, astonishment vivid on his face. 'I'm not sure I've ever been summed up quite like that before.'

But she wasn't backing down. She straightened and drained her glass. 'What did the last woman you subjugated like to call it?'

His lips twisted and his eyes darkened and, in that moment, the little corner he'd backed her into shrunk just like Wonderland around Alice. Yet he still found room to take one more half step forward.

'The last woman I subjugated begged me to do it,' he breathed. His eyes flicked down and he stretched out a finger and ran the knuckle down the laces of her arty bustier.

Instant heat rushed up into her chest and bloomed tellingly in her décolletage.

She twisted away from his cloying presence and crossed back to the bar. 'Nice try.' She laughed, one-hundred-per-cent casual and two-hundred-per-cent fake, and signalled the bartender for a repeat of her drink. 'But I'm not buying it.'

He was right behind her. 'Buying what?'

'All of it. The charming, rich bad-boy act, the overbearing son, the interfering business partner.'

'Are you saying I'm not all those things?'

'Oh, you're definitely all of them, but I don't buy that that's *all* you are. There's something else going on. I'll just have to work out what it is.'

'I'm no mystery, Tash. What you see is what you get.'

She turned to face him. 'You're in business, Aiden. What you see is never what you get.' She glanced around. 'Now if you'll excuse me, there's someone over there I'm sure I should meet.'

She spun, skirts flowing, and left him standing speechless in her wake.

Tash Sinclair worked the room like a professional. Ten days ago, he would have imagined the wrong kind of professional, but now he watched her through a different lens. A Tash-coloured lens. One not quite so tinted by what he thought he knew.

She'd summed him up so accurately earlier this evening, nailed him to the cross of his own bad behaviour and then promptly ignored him for the next two hours. She flitted from guest to guest charming the men, engaging the women and drafting them into the ranks of Team Tash. She was exactly as she promised him to be: intriguing enough to have multiple curious eyes follow her around the room, but appropriate enough to give the tabloids nothing tangible—or even intangible—to work with. She'd brushed past his father several times and the glances they exchanged were carefully neutral, blank enough to give no cause for comment whatsoever.

Unless you were looking for cause.

Or was he still digging for something that just wasn't there? Reacting to a decades-old incident that he still didn't fully understand. Something had happened twenty years ago, something that had created tension in his extended family and a wedge between his parents. Something to do with a woman. And he'd grown up with the echoes of that event and the memory of his mother sobbing in the wine cellar where she'd gone not to be heard and cursing a name he'd only ever heard whispered by his aunts and uncles thereafter.

Porter.

That was all he knew. But it was enough to teach him an early lesson about fidelity. And about how many different things a man could be at the same time. Successful businessman. Loving father. Cheating husband. He'd learned to compartmentalise the same way his mother presumably had in order to continue living with—and loving—the man that could do something like that. They'd worked their way through it and onto another twenty years of marriage and Aiden had, too.

But he'd never forgotten it. Or the lessons it taught him about trust.

His eyes tracked Tash the length of the room.

'She's something else, isn't she?' The voice came out of nowhere, low and edgy to his left. 'Have you slept with her yet?'

Aiden spun to face the question.

'Something to look forward to,' the man went on. 'She's a cracker.'

The disrespect and sheer contempt in Kyle Jardine's eyes stabbed in below Aiden's ribs. Hard and ugly. His curiosity hardened up into pure anger. 'Harsh words considering you got rich off her back, Jardine.'

The mayor's eyes narrowed. 'Or she got rich *on* hers. Though, to be fair, she was on top more often than not.'

The urgent need to defend Tash slammed headlong into the unbidden image of her, all golden and glorious reared back above him. Jardine's words should have been exactly what he wanted to hear. That she was the gold-digger he'd always suspected. That she'd slept her way to her present success.

Except, inexplicably, he didn't believe that. Not for one moment.

That just wasn't Tash.

'I didn't realise you were on the list for tonight,' Aiden muttered, knowing full well Jardine wasn't. Though it had been tempting to get him along to pick his brains about Tash. Turned out there wasn't much brain there to pick amongst.

'Admin error, I'm sure. I came with Shannon Carles.'

Right. His latest 'cracker'.

'I hadn't realised exactly who your father's ingénue was,' Jardine went on, blind to the tension pouring off Aiden. 'Should I give him a heads-up that there's not too much that's innocent about her?' He shoved his hands deep into his pockets and Aiden had never had a stronger urge to step slightly away.

His fingers curled into fists of their own accord. 'Her personal life is none of MooreCo's concern. We've simply commissioned her artistic skills.'

'I give that a week.' Jardine snorted, swigging down the last of his drink. 'She's insidious.'

If he'd said anything else…any other word…

'What do you mean?' The question bled out of him. So maybe at least one part of him was still looking for evidence.

'You won't mean to. You won't know quite how it happened. But one day you'll have her toothbrush in your cabinet and her brand of milk in your fridge.'

'That doesn't sound too sinister.' It actually sounded weirdly good. For a half a heartbeat.

'She's like one of those spiders that lures you in with the pretty exoskeleton and the seductive dance and then, once she's got you, *wham*, not so pretty and not so seductive any more.'

He couldn't really imagine either of those things. 'She doesn't strike me as the black widow type.'

'I'm talking about the tears and the neediness that start.'

Needy. Hadn't he used the exact same word himself, earlier? Aiden stared at Jardine and wondered if this was how *he* came across to strangers. Or, worse, to people he knew.

Maybe to Tash.

'Classic bait and switch, mate,' Jardine said, turning for the bar. 'That's all I'm saying.'

No. He was saying so much more, and he was probably saying it to everyone here. Suddenly those eyes following Tash around the room didn't seem so benign. He scanned the venue, found Jardine's date drinking it up at the second bar and reached for his phone.

He and Carles had at least two mutual friends. One of them was bound to owe him a favour.

Within ten minutes, Carles was shoving her mobile phone back into her purse and copping an earful from a very unhappy Jardine as they moved towards the exit. He couldn't really stay without his date and she'd just received an urgent phone call from her marketing department....

Unfortunate, but necessary, she'd gushed.

Aiden had just smiled and held the door for them both.

As he turned back to the room he caught the tail end of Tash's glance. Her relief was patent and he knew, without asking, that Jardine had likely been enjoying taunting her with his presence.

'Jerk,' he muttered.

'I hope that wasn't for me, darling,' a familiar voice said from behind him.

He turned into the warmth of a familiar smile. 'Mother.'

'Well, I'm here. I hope this will be worth it,' she announced. It had been years since Laura Moore had been to any of MooreCo's events. The ribbon-cutting for the Terrace high-rise was probably the last. Corporate parties, unlike dinner ones, just weren't his mother's forte. She didn't do well with all that pressure and no formal role to play.

'Thank you for coming,' he murmured, kissing her cheek. Though his purpose for asking wasn't quite as solid now as it had been at eight o'clock this morning. This morning he'd believed that his mother's presence might help to remind Tash that Nathaniel Moore had a loving wife to go home to. That there was a marriage about to be wrecked. And it might help his father, too, to have them in the same room at the same time. For the same reasons.

Maybe that was all he needed to be cured of this obsession he seemed to have.

Insidious. An ugly word from an ugly human being but he just couldn't shake it. Tash had certainly wheedled her way dangerously close to *out* of his bad books, which was quite an achievement given how *in them* she'd been when he first walked into her studio.

He furnished his mother with something from the bar, topped up his own glass and then turned to search out his father.

'Who's your father talking to?'

Aiden's heart shrivelled to half its size as his eyes followed the direction of his mother's enquiry, but then plumped out again as he realised it wasn't Tash. 'Margaret Osborne. The wife of—'

'Trevor Osborne, yes, I recognise her now. Goodness, the years haven't been kind.'

Every part of him cringed at the slightly too-loud tenor of her voice. Guess that was what came of being out of the scene for so long—she'd lost her social skills when it came to business matters. Though he couldn't even imagine her working a room quite as fearlessly as Tash, even at the top of her game.

He shepherded his mother across the crowded room until they caught his father's eye. It widened with alarm—as well it might....

'Laura?'

She leaned in for an air kiss—so she hadn't completely forgotten how to be Mrs Nathaniel Moore—and then smiled at her husband's surprise. 'I know. I'm as flummoxed to be here as you are seeing me. Your junior partner invited me.'

His father seemed about as discomposed as Aiden had ever seen him. 'You're always invited, Laura. You know that.' Dark eyes scanned the room and then flared even further.

'Nathaniel, should we—?' Tash appeared by Aiden's side and then jerked to a halt at the immediate tension in his father's body language. 'Oh, I'm sorry for interrupting.'

She turned her curiosity to his mother, who stood politely blank-faced.

His father quite literally couldn't speak.

'Laura Moore,' his mother finally said, introducing herself on a smile, her dark brows slightly folded in. 'And you are?'

'I'm—' Tash opened her mouth to speak but both men rushed to cut her off.

'The guest of honour,' Nathaniel said.

'Natasha's here with me,' Aiden blurted, simultaneously. The surprise Tash turned on him very neatly matched his own. Why the hell had he said that? Was it because inviting his mother here tonight suddenly seemed like the worst idea ever?

Or was it because he didn't want to be proved correct all of a sudden?

'Oh, you're the artist?' Laura covered for both her momentarily inept men. 'Nathaniel has brought home photographs of your work. Just lovely.'

Tash smiled and Aiden recognised it instantly as her *game-face* smile. The one she'd been feeding everyone here. The one she'd used with him the first few times they met. The fact that she couldn't be genuinely polite to the wife of her biggest commissioner instantly brought his suspicion screaming back to the fore.

Why not—what did she have to lose? Or hide?

But her answer gave nothing away. 'Thank you, Mrs Moore.'

'Please, call me Laura.'

That offer seemed to actually pain Tash, but she kept the fake smile glued to her face. Was he the only one who could see how it paled just slightly at the corners?

His own frown deepened until it must have matched his mother's.

'Have we met?' Laura queried. 'You seem so familiar….'

'I don't think so,' Nathaniel cut in. 'Perhaps in the newspapers?'

'Perhaps.' She pressed steepled fingers to her lips and it was the first time his mother had struck him as old. But compared to the golden, smooth skin of the woman by her side, the wrinkles on his mother's hands cried out with obviousness. 'Never mind, it will come to me.'

'A drink, Laura?' Nathaniel asked.

Everyone's eyes went instantly to the glass of wine already in his wife's hands. Okay, it was official…he'd *never* seen his father this ruffled.

'Tash has quite a rare talent,' Aiden murmured, to cover his father's gaffe. He'd wanted to throw the spectre of 'the wife' in between Tash and his father, not cause his mother any further pain, and his father's sputtering was only going to pique her curiosity and have her asking questions she might not like the answer to. 'Her work is going to make such a statement at the entrance to MooreCo.'

Tash turned her surprise to him. 'Thank you, Aiden. I think that might be the first nice thing you've said about me.'

'Your work is beautiful,' he hedged.

She laughed. Right when he expected her lips to purse up tight. 'I'll still take it. I get the feeling praise is a rare thing from you.'

His mother's eyes immediately honed in on her, and immediately jumped to the wrong conclusion. Or the right one given he'd just, stupidly, declared her to be his date. She turned positively conspiratorial. 'He's a Moore, Natasha. You could die waiting for a pleased word....'

Tash's laugh-lines immediately reconfigured into a complicated little cluster of confusion. Perhaps it was easier for her to do what she was doing if she imagined that Laura Moore was a cold, distant wife.

Far from the truth.

Certainly his father seemed unable to countenance them speaking directly to each other.

'Perhaps it's time for the speeches, Tash?'

She turned, bestowed the only genuine smile of the night on his father and then excused herself. As soon as both of them began making their way towards the small stage, his mother rounded on him. 'An artistic type, Aiden? That's very *un*-you.'

There was a reason for that. 'Perhaps I just don't meet arty types, usually.'

'She seems very sweet.'

'That *would* be very un-me. Besides, how would you know? The two of you barely spoke a word.'

'I don't need to converse with her to know. I could practically feel the electricity coming off the pair of you.'

Or perhaps she was just misreading the source of whatever she'd sensed. Maybe the sparks were the energy zinging back and forth between Tash and his father. And maybe that was what caused the apparent short fuse in his father's brain.

'Bring her for dinner.'

Into his parents' home? *Uh, no.* Not going to happen.

The lights around them dimmed, triggering a reluctant hush to fall over the liquored-up crowd. His father stepped up onto stage, drawing Tash in his wake. She stood right on the edge of the lit area of the stage, polite and demure but impossible to take your eyes off. Even doing nothing, she was intriguing. The blonde flare of her hair, the single streak of perfectly positioned, artistically oriented burgundy sweeping down across her smooth forehead. Artful smudges around her eyes and very little else on the intelligent face focused entirely on his father. And then the open expanse of creamy shoulders and chest above the patterned bustier that kept her cleavage firmly restrained behind a zip. The light fairly glowed off her unmarked skin and it was all too easy imagining lowering that convenient zip to see if the skin beneath was as pristine.

'The light favours her,' his mother whispered, her gaze correctly tracking his to its destination.

It galled him to hear her compliment the woman who was stealing her husband's focus. He pressed his lips together and forced his attention off the woman practically glowing on-stage and onto his father. 'I think she just knows how to use it,' he murmured.

'It's not like your father to be so discomposed. Perhaps it's because I'm here? Or perhaps he has some secret lover tucked away behind the scenes?'

Aiden laughed where he was supposed to—a tight, short chuckle—and focused on his father's face. The tense, formal man before them wasn't a shade of the relaxed, casual man of a few hours ago. Of just ten minutes ago. It contrasted awkwardly with the beautiful, flowing images of Tash's glass design glowing on the big screen behind him.

'…and so, without further ado, I give you the creative spirit behind MooreCo's newest acquisition—' he took a long breath in, found his wife in the darkened crowd and braved her curious stare '—Natasha Sinclair.'

The audience's burst of applause almost drowned out his mother's gasp, but Aiden felt it in the stiffening of her body where it pressed against his side in the crush. He tore his eyes from Tash long enough to look down on his mother's pale face. Her lips made a straight, devastated line in her face but her eyes were busy, flicking back and forth between her husband and his ingénue.

Tash started speaking, and her disarming cadence had the audience enraptured as she described the creative intent behind her thalassic theme, but it did nothing to lessen the tension pouring off his mother. He turned with her as her body spun away and he hurried to follow her outside.

'Mum…?'

Something major was going on. Something he was starting to wish he understood before the flawed brilliance of inviting his mother here tonight.

'I take it back,' she choked, hurrying down the steps to the old building. 'Do not bring that woman to dinner.'

That woman. He'd heard that phrase before. When no one knew he was listening. But Tash would have been a little girl when that phrase was first whispered between his mother and her siblings. She simply couldn't be *that woman.*

'What's going on, Mum?'

'Was it not bad enough twenty years ago?' she half raged.

'Now he brings her back into our lives this way through her cheap daughter. God, I *knew* I recognised her from somewhere....'

He reached out and caught his mother by the arm. 'Calm down. Stop. Tell me what the problem is.'

'I'll tell you exactly who the problem is, Aiden.' Her chest rose and fell with pained regularity. 'It's your *date*.'

She peered up at him with the kind of motherly authority and blatant agony that no son could stomach. 'Natasha?'

'Did you know who she was when you asked me along tonight?'

Guilt raged from cell to cell in his body. He *had* brought her here tonight to shake things up a bit. But he'd had no idea that he was setting his mother up for this kind of hurt. And, deep down, he didn't believe that his father and Tash had done anything wrong. Yet. Certainly not enough to be upsetting his mother to this degree.

'She's Natasha Sinclair. An artist—' he started.

The snort of derision was immediate and unfamiliar in his genteel mother and it morphed into a half-sob. 'She may be a Sinclair, but she's also a *Porter*.'

CHAPTER FOUR

'"He knew my mother..."' Aiden snarled, shunting Tash back into the tiny coat-filled room with his big body. He slammed the door on prying ears and locked it.

She literally recoiled from the ugly accusation in his handsome face and shrugged back a few more inches into the protection of the expensive coats all around her. 'Aiden, what—?'

'We had a fifteen-minute wait for the taxi I called because Mum was too hysterical to drive. She shared the whole sordid story. All about your mother's affair with my father. I never would have invited her if I'd known.'

'Is she all right?'

His lips flattened. 'No. You do not get to play the gracious innocent party. Her sister is en route to meet her at home and try and repair the damage you've done here tonight.'

'I've done? You invited her.'

'You hunted us down. Forced your way into my family's lives. None of this would have happened if not for that.'

'That's not what—'

But he wasn't listening. Of course he wasn't. He was a Moore. 'In my family we know her as Porter,' he barged on. 'Why?'

The he-man thing was getting old. Tash stood up taller and gained some return ground on him. 'In *your family* she was a pariah, and you lot made her life miserable!' she hissed.

'Porter was her maiden name. That's what they knew her as at uni.'

'University? But that was years before.'

'That's how they met. They were all in the same year. My mother and yours. They were friends.'

'Friends?' That took him aback. 'I guess I shouldn't be surprised at your behaviour, then, if that's the kind of treacherous stock you come from.'

She stepped up to him hard. Peered up into all that anger and ignored the cheap, ugly shot at her. 'Your father cheated, too.'

'Oh, I have a whole other conversation waiting for him, don't you worry. This is about you.'

'Why? I was seven years old when they...' She couldn't bring herself to say the word. *Affair*. Besides, did the word even apply if it was only one weekend? Although deep down she knew that their love affair had gone on for decades regardless of only being together the once.

He glared down on her. 'Guilty by association. Why are you in our lives now? Why suddenly emerge?'

'Because *she died*, Aiden. And she died still loving your father.' She swallowed back the choke. 'I just wanted to know the man that held her heart all these years.'

He struggled with that news. 'Why stir it all up?'

'I wasn't stirring anything. I only wanted to meet him, talk to him. Try to get some closure for both of them. *You* were the one that forced the issue of the commission and dragged me into your lives. *You* were the one that brought your mother here tonight and ripped the decades-old scab off it all.'

He didn't look as if her being right made the truth any easier to swallow. He practically scraped around for an out and found it in picking a fight. 'You looked at her like you didn't like her.'

'Why would I like the woman that helped make my mother's life a misery? Why would I like any of you? You Moores trashed the Porter name any chance you got. She was practically ostracised from her community because of you all.'

He glared down on her. 'Leave me out of it. I was the same age as you.'

'Right. So neither of us was responsible—we're just left picking up the pieces.'

He *so* looked as if he wanted to keep arguing but the logic of her argument was hard to refute. His nostrils flared twice before his body sagged. 'You just wanted to meet him?'

'I needed to. Her diaries were full of him. I wanted to give them both that closure.'

'That's why he's so obsessed with you?'

It hit her then. Exactly why Aiden Moore thought she was spending so much time around his father. 'Isn't it bad enough you thought I was chasing him? Now you think we were actually on together?' The thought would have been vaguely disturbing if not for the obvious truth. 'I'm a shadow of an obsession. A last chance at something he once wanted so badly.'

'You're talking about my father, Tash.'

'I know. And I'm sorry. It affects my family, too, but it doesn't change the truth. They were in love. They just could never be together.'

'Together enough to get caught.'

She had to remember this news was just minutes old for Aiden. She'd had much longer to come to terms with the whole sorry mess. 'They weren't caught. Your father confessed.'

'What do you mean?'

'The one time they acted on it. He regretted betraying his promise to your mother. So he told her what he'd done, and never saw my mother again.'

Though, in truth, he'd been betraying Laura Moore his

whole life by loving someone else secretly. And betraying himself by not acting on it.

Poor Nathaniel. Poor Laura. Her poor mother. Not one happy person in the whole sorry mess.

'Did she tell your father?'

Tash dropped her eyes. 'No. He found out through mutual friends.' Not how she would have done it herself, but then she'd never been trapped in violence the way her mother had with an angry, gutless man.

'Lack of character must run in the family.'

She shoved his chest, hard; loyalty blazing hot and live in her heart. 'You can take all the shots you want at me, but don't you dare impugn a woman who can no longer defend herself or her actions.'

He didn't respond, but his eyes darkened two shades and blazed down into hers. Her shove hadn't even budged his feet from the tips of hers. 'She must have been something, your mother,' he breathed down on her. 'To inspire such passion in her child. To inspire such treachery in my father.'

'She was an *amazing* woman. And it takes two to tango. Especially horizontally.'

His hand moved up to finger a stray lock of hair back to the safety of its fellows and her mind filled with images of her and Aiden getting horizontal. Her chest tightened instantly.

'You really believe that.'

'I really do,' she breathed. 'I'm sorry that it has caused pain for your family but I'm not sorry my mother got a single weekend of heaven in what was otherwise a pretty miserable existence.'

'She loved him that much?'

'She lived for him.' Until the day she just couldn't live any longer, even for him.

Aiden dropped his forehead and let his eyes squeeze shut.

Tash tried to remember that his world—his family—had just imploded.

'Do you want to drop the commission?' she asked after an age.

'No.' Those blue-grey eyes snapped open. It was almost as if the word had fallen off his lips without his consent. 'We have a contract. Besides, the next step is up to my father. This is his mess. If he asks you to go, will you?'

It hurt having her mother's memory summed up as a mess. 'If he asks me. Yes.'

But he wouldn't. Her mother's memory was too strong. Although, if staying led to Nathaniel getting hurt she'd definitely go regardless of what he wanted.

'You are such a paradox,' Aiden murmured, leaning his weight back onto the old counter. His expensive suit cuffs pulled up as he crossed his arms across his chest. 'Jardine called you insidious.'

'Kyle's a mean drunk.'

'But he's not wrong.'

Her heart sank. Really? *Him too*? Somehow, she'd hoped for better from the son of the man her mother had loved. Which was probably stupid.

'There's something about you….' Aiden went on. 'It's hard to put my finger on.' But he did, tracing it along the top edge of her bodice.

Her throat tightened up immediately and the *thing* between them surged and swelled as a ball of heat low in her chest. There it was again…the connection. So ready to combust. 'Two minutes ago you were angry.'

'I'm still angry. Just not at you, specifically.'

'And two minutes ago you thought I was sleeping with your father.'

He shuffled closer. 'But you're not. And my relief about that is quite…disturbing.'

'Why relieved?' She didn't dare ask *why disturbed*....

'Because it means I can do this.'

The warmth of the cumulative coats hanging at her back was nothing to the furnace pumping off Aiden as he swooped down to capture her lips with his. They took hers with a certainty that stole her breath. As if he knew exactly how well they'd fit together and how welcome he would be. And how little resistance she'd give him. He pressed hard against her and held her firm with strong arms banded around behind her.

Every sultry look, every snark, every narrow-eyed glare he'd given her had been leading to this moment. Tash wondered if he knew it as well as she did. She'd felt it back in that café, the first time he'd passed her table.

She wanted to respond to him—his size, his intensity and the sheer overwhelming maleness of him—but something told her if she gave an inch, she'd be lost. Aiden Moore was a man who knew what he wanted and how he wanted it.

And right now, the answers were *her* and *here in the coatroom of MooreCo's party.*

As if he sensed her slight withdrawal, his fingers stole up and tangled in her cropped hair, making gentle fists in the shaggy locks and then pulling on it, strong and steady until her throat was bared to the ravages of his lips. The touch of dominance sent her blood racing even faster and made her squirm against his hard body. His mouth feasted on her throat, one big hand sliding down to bunch a fistful of skirt up under her bottom.

Every part of her responded to his magnetic pull. It would be so easy just to slip her arms up around his neck and hold on as he kissed her half to death. It would be just as easy to let him lift her up onto the original timber counter in this old building and wrap her legs around him, too.

'Won't this be tough to explain to your mother?' she gasped between kisses. If she was thinking more clearly, she might also have spared a brain cell or two as to how his father might take the news.

'I don't generally get her to sign off on who I'm sleeping with.' He pressed the words against her ear.

'You assume I'll be sleeping with you,' she breathed.

'Oh, you will,' he bit against her lips. 'Besides, it's not like you'll ever be coming to a family dinner or anything.'

He meant because of their family situation. She knew that. But the stark reality was enough to pull her completely out of the sensual fog robbing her of strength. She'd promised herself she'd never be treated like that again.

He lifted his lids to reveal glazed eyes. 'What?'

She brought both hands around and pressed them into his chest with as much certainty as he'd kissed her. It opened up precious air between them. Not much, but enough. 'We can't do this.'

'You mean not here?'

'I mean not at all.'

'But you're not sleeping with my father....'

As if *his* issues were the only ones standing between them. 'I work for you, now.'

'So?'

'So it's inappropriate.' That concept clearly had never occurred to him. 'And it's too messy, politically.'

He stepped in closer. Smiled in that Cheshire cat way. 'I was counting on it being messy.'

'Aiden, stop.' She pushed him harder and he staggered back all of an inch.

But he did stop. Exactly when it mattered. 'You're serious?'

'Of course I'm serious. Did you think I was just playing hard to get?'

His brows folded in. 'Well…yeah. Is it because it's too public?'

Actually, the risk of someone knocking on that door made

the whole thing even more breathless than it might otherwise have been. It wasn't why she was stopping.

'It's because it's too…close.' She took a deep breath. 'You and I getting together never would have worked. Plus I barely know you.'

'You know my family. You know where I work. You know what I like for lunch and how I take my bourbon. And you know what happens when our pheromones start mixing. What more is there?'

And that was probably exactly how it worked in his world. The world where relationships were days long. 'Other things. Normal things.' Lord, what she wouldn't give to be treated like something to be treasured instead of conquered or leveraged. Just for once. 'But it's a moot point. This—' she gestured back and forth between them '—isn't going to happen.'

'All those reasons you just gave me for why not can be addressed by the same thing.' The fact he was helping her straighten her skirt was the only reason she wasn't shoving him away harder. 'We keep it quiet. Only meet privately. Then no problem.'

She stared at him. God, the male mind was a complex, beautiful and totally naive thing. 'It's still a problem. It's just hidden.'

And dishonest. And cheap. And she was through with feeling cheap.

His hiss reflected his expression exactly.

She sat back and regarded him. 'You don't hear "no" very often, do you?'

His laugh mocked. 'I'm not going to cry, if that's what you're thinking. Or beg.'

'I can't even begin to imagine what that would look like.'

He stared at her in silence. Refixed his tie.

'You strike me as the sort who only wants me because you can't have me,' she said, wrestling her breath under control.

'Is that right?'

'Isn't it?'

His eyes narrowed and he glared at her, failing abysmally at intimidating her. Strangely, she realised, she held all the power here.

Lord, how he must hate that.

She finally broke the silence. 'So now what?'

'Now you walk out of here well ahead of me.'

She laughed. 'Suddenly you're concerned for my reputation?'

He smiled and opened the door wide for her. Wide enough to exit but narrow enough that she had to press against him. She did so with the greatest care. But as she squeezed her body past his, his lips brushed her ear for half a heartbeat, and his warm breath caused a riot in her nerve endings.

'Not yours, Tash...'

Aiden watched Tash stride confidently out of that little room and knew she was faking it. She was as shaken as he was by what had just happened.

He could see it in her eyes.

But was she shaken by what *he'd* done, or by what *she'd* done? That was the question.

The part of his mind that should have been dealing with what he'd discovered about his family tonight was in lock-down, but, as it always had, a good physical distraction helped him to suppress the thoughts until a more appropriate time. A time when he wasn't surrounded by their colleagues. A time when he wasn't going to have to face his father, smile and be the picture-perfect son.

Or, if he got lucky, he'd suppress it enough that he wouldn't have to face it at all. Done was done, dissecting it wasn't going to change a thing.

Lord knew that was how it was done in the Moore family. If you worked hard enough at ignoring something then it just…ceased to be. The status quo eventually returned without anyone having to strip themselves raw emotionally.

You just had to wait it out.

He'd only ever seen his mother as she was tonight once before. Though that time he'd not *seen* her, only heard her through the ventilation system as she wailed her heart out down in the wine cellar while he crouched next to his child's bed with its Batman linen, his arms circling his knees, ear pressed to the air vent in his room. That was twenty-odd years ago. So he didn't know what to do tonight when the mother that he adored fell apart right in front of him, other than get her the hell out of there and then get really, really angry.

And hunt for an outlet.

And Tash's infallible logic had robbed him of the outlet he'd planned to have, so he changed tack and redirected it.

Kissing her was a much better idea all round. Firing her blood and bending her to his will was both intensely satisfying and fantastic selective anaesthesia. It simply wasn't possible for him to feel anguish and desire at the same time. It numbed all the parts that he didn't want to think about and stimulated all the parts he liked to think about most.

And it caused the deep chocolate of Tash's eyes to first spit with resistance and then melt with passion. As always, he'd loved the power implicit in the moment that happened. And he loved her capitulation even more for being such an intriguing mix of resignation and anticipation.

Until she'd turned the tables on him, of course.

'Son…'

He tacked away from his father and headed for the bar. 'Later, Dad.'

'We need to talk.'

No. They really didn't. What they needed was to be far

apart for as long as it took for the wounds to start scabbing over. Then they'd see. 'Later,' he cut back over his shoulder.

His father slowed to a stop and Aiden could feel his eyes boring into his back as he ordered the largest bourbon the barman would serve him. That was pretty good selective anaesthesia, too.

He took a healthy swig and turned to face his father, but he'd disappeared into the partying crowd.

His eyes scanned the room, searching for someone else. For a slash of Nordic blonde hair. When he found her, Tash was doing a bang-up job of ignoring him, but he sensed that she knew exactly where he was. She laughed and smiled as she spoke with some of MooreCo's less controversial clients but—even from across the room—he could see the smile was a thin veneer.

And it pleased him—bastard that he was—to know that he was responsible for its fragility. Just to know he had any kind of impact on her at all.

That was a satisfactory revenge for the fact that, while he might have set out to distract Tash from his father with faux interest, somewhere along the line the interest had grown very, very real.

CHAPTER FIVE

TASH DRAGGED HER eyes back from the crowded football stadium beyond the triple-glazed windows and focused back on Nathaniel, who was just settling back into his seat after leaping to his feet at the hard-won goal down on the field.

'So you never told him?'

Nathaniel tugged at the bottom of his jacket, and his eyes drifted across the crowded corporate box to Aiden chatting to two men over by the table laden with a luscious seafood spread. 'How could I? He's my son.'

Tash lowered her voice despite knowing Aiden would never hear them in the noisy room on the other side of the glass. 'But he found out anyway?'

'He was such a quiet child, people tended to say more than they should in front of him.'

Quiet? Aiden? That wasn't an image she could easily conjure. 'What else was he like?'

Nathaniel's eyes narrowed just slightly at the direction of her question, but then softened at the corners and refocused thirty years over her shoulder. 'He was a spectacular boy. Thoughtful and considerate. Keen to learn. Focused. His quiet nature meant he thought about things deeply, even then.'

Thoughtful and considerate? 'What happened?'

It was only as the words tumbled off her lips that Tash realised how insensitive they were.

'Don't misjudge him, Tash. Aiden feels things passionately and he has such a refined sense of right and wrong. Sometimes those things come into conflict.'

'Does that include his father now?' Nathaniel's eyes dropped. 'I know you're staying in a hotel. Are you also avoiding the office?' Or is he? They were only at this football game together because they had guests who expected to see both of them. The happy front.

He shook his head with determination. 'He's grown up with all the murmurs and none of the facts.'

See, now…this was what a father was supposed to do. Defend his child against everything. Even the hint of criticism. *This* was how it should be. Something she'd never had from Eric Sinclair. It was hard not to covet it just a little bit.

'Did you ever think about telling him once he was an adult?' she asked once the roar of the crowd for a goal well kicked settled.

'His good opinion means too much to me.'

'You had to know he'd find out…. Your wife too.' If not last week then…some time.

He nodded. 'I knew. Maybe I thought I could delay it, control it.' He stared some place over her shoulder. 'Bring things to a head at long last.'

Insight flooded into her. 'You wanted this.'

His groan drowned under the cheers of another brilliant on-field play. Tash saw it in the slump of his shoulders more than heard it. 'I wanted it revealed. Exposed.' His eyes lifted. 'Denying your mother broke something in me. She's beyond harm now. I can finally acknowledge us. I can finally acknowledge *her*.'

After thirty years of holding it in.

Sorrow-drenched eyes lifted to hers. 'I've used you, Tash. But I didn't mean for it to hurt you. I'm so sorry.'

'You haven't caused me any harm.' Unlike his son. 'But I am sorry for what it means for your marriage.'

He sighed heavily. 'That's for Laura and me to sort out. My marriage has been flawed for a very long time. Twice I failed to have the strength to do what I should have. Maybe I've finally grown up.'

She almost missed it, so casually was it uttered. Yet her mother's diaries attested to them never seeing each other again after that one time two decades ago.

'Twice?' she risked.

He smiled and patted her hand. 'No, I kept my word to Laura. I haven't seen your mother since you were young. I meant before. At university.'

She frowned. 'I don't understand.'

He matched her confusion. 'Your mother and I were an item before I was with Laura.'

'What?' Tash sat up straight. 'Why wasn't that in her diaries?'

He measured his words as he thought that through. 'Perhaps your father. He was a petty and jealous man. My mere name enraged him. Maybe she feared he would read her diaries?'

Yes. He was absolutely the sort to do that. And to take out that anger on her mother. 'But then you were together, and she wrote about that.' If she hadn't, Tash wouldn't have known about any of it.

'She'd left him by the time she wrote about it. I remember her saying, once, that she left blank pages in the diary where I would be.'

'So she went back and wrote it in?'

'I assume so. Once she was safe to.'

Safe. So he knew. Anxiety churned over in her stomach. She wanted to ask but knew it would be an accusation. 'How could you leave her with him?' she whispered. 'Knowing how violent he was?'

His skin blanched. 'I acted as soon as I knew for sure. But Adele refused to let me expose myself. The most I could do was give her the money she needed to get the two of you away from him. And arrange the trigger.'

Tash studied the awkwardness of his expression. The careful way his eyes avoided her. 'Trigger?'

Nathaniel blew out a long breath. 'I made sure that Eric found out about us. To force his hand. Your mother never knew.'

The accidental slip by her mother's sister suddenly made more sense. Not accidental at all. But her father didn't like Aunt Karen and so would totally have bought the apparent betrayal. And revelled in it. 'But then you *were* exposed.'

His eyes were so earnest. So very intent. 'I didn't care about my reputation. I just wanted her safe. And you, too.'

And maybe he'd wanted to bring things to a head even two decades ago. So he'd manufactured the trigger and funded her mother's escape and the cottage they'd moved straight into. Did Laura know that?

'So...what happened at university, then? Why didn't you stay together?' If the love was so deep.

He shrugged. 'Aiden was conceived.'

She wasn't quick enough to moderate the inward suck of her shock. 'You slept with Laura while you were seeing my mother?'

'No.' The fierceness of his denial threw her. Considering it was coming from a man who'd cheated on his wife. 'We broke up for three weeks over something stupid but in that time I...' His colour rose. 'I was a child for all I thought I knew about the world. I slept with Laura to make a statement.'

Oh, God. 'And she got pregnant.'

'She did.'

Instant karma. 'When did you find out?'

'About a month after your mother and I got back together.'

'And you stood by Laura?'

His back straightened. 'I got her pregnant. It was the eighties.'

Exactly; not the fifties. But Nathaniel Moore was old school in some ways. And maybe his honour was as twisted as his son's. 'And Mum?'

'Devastated.' As you would be. 'I don't think she ever would have become involved with Eric if I hadn't hurt her so badly.'

'You blame yourself.'

'Every day for the past thirty years.'

'But you don't blame Aiden?' Where did that come from? And why did she care what kind of relationship was between the two men?

Nathaniel studied her closely. 'Tash. I hope you're not entertaining thoughts of…Aiden and you would not be a good fit.'

The low blow got her hackles up. That kind of attitude was not something she expected from this man, so disappointment bit low and sharp. 'Not good enough for the Moore heir, Nathaniel?

His eyes hardened. 'You know me better than that. He should be lucky to find a woman as intelligent and talented and good as you.'

The betrayal stung. For Aiden. 'He's your son.'

'That's right, he is. And so I'm in the best position to suggest that he's a bad fit for someone with your softness. I just think you can do…better,' he urged, unnaturally intent.

Awkwardness saturated the air around them for the first time. 'Well, you don't have to worry. We don't have that kind of relationship.'

'Promise me you won't get involved with him. On your mother's memory.'

Images of heady kisses amongst luxury coats skittered through her mind. But her mother's memory was not something she could take lightly. 'I promise I will never settle for less than I believe I'm worth. How's that?'

Not good enough, judging by the shadow that struck across his gaze. 'Tash—'

'Sorry to interrupt,' a thoroughly unamused voice said from behind. 'Richard was hoping to get a few moments of your attention some time today.'

Nathaniel straightened as stiffly as if he'd been caught ensconced in conversation with Adele rather than her daughter. Tash used the moment it took him to push to his feet to brush away her confusion at what had just passed.

Nathaniel warning her thoroughly off his son. Was Aiden really that damaged?

'Yes. Of course,' he said.

Nathaniel excused himself and quietly closed the glass door between the viewing room and the socialising room behind him. Neither man met the other's eyes as they passed. Aiden gifted all his concentration to the football game proceeding far below in the stadium, then turned to stare at his father, inside.

Pain reflected back at him from the glass.

Watching two men who loved each other drift so far apart was awful.

'How are you doing?' Tash risked after a tense silence.

His answer was only a nod, but at least he tossed that in her direction. 'How's the piece coming along?'

'Very well. It's shaping up to be quite something.'

More silence. *Excellent.*

But before she could break it, he turned and spoke directly to her for the first time in days. 'You know, you don't need to feign interest in things to spend time with him. He's not going anywhere now that he's found you.'

Tash sighed to discover they were still no closer to a truce than before. 'I'm not feigning anything.'

'You don't strike me as an Aussie Rules fan.'

'This is my team. I used to come with my mother. I love football.'

'Uh-huh.'

'You find that hard to believe?'

'You're more WAG territory than fan territory. And you laugh at his jokes constantly. You're telling me that's not a bit sycophantic?'

Tash frowned. What was going on? 'We share a sense of humour.'

'You've even adopted some of his mannerisms.'

'What mannerisms?'

'That one there, for starters. The single brow-lift when challenged.'

Oh, for crying out loud. 'Me and half the world.'

'You're playing up to him.'

She curled her fingers at the side where he couldn't see them. 'No. I'm not. We just have things in common.'

'Carefully engineered things.'

'Why would I do that?'

'To draw him closer. To reel him in.'

She let the insult slide. Those she was used to. 'To what end? You've already said he's not going anywhere.'

'I don't know. Maybe just shoring up your place in his life?'

Or *Aiden's* place, perhaps. Something about the turmoil behind his eyes hit her then. A trace of desperation. In a man who'd negotiated as many big deals as Aiden had, that was a careless tell. She stood and crossed to his side by the viewing window.

'Aiden, look…' He turned a baleful expression on her. 'I

can see how bad things are between your father and you and I know how that must feel—'

'Oh, you know? Really?'

Actually yes, she did. As a woman who'd spent her childhood trying to be good enough to please her father.

She tried again. 'I'm sure it's easier to target your anger on me—'

'You don't think you've earned my displeasure?'

'We were both kids, then—'

'I'm not talking about then. I'm talking about now.'

'What am I doing that's making you so mad?'

'You're flirting with him.'

Seriously? This again? 'I'm not—'

'I'm not saying it's sexual, but you're hovering, keeping him on your hook.'

'I'm—'

'What hope does he have of getting things sorted between him and my mother if you're hanging around reminding him of *her*?'

Colour flared up his neck and her heart squeezed. It was slow to fill again.

She lowered her voice. 'Is that what you want? For them to sort things out?'

He stepped dangerously closer and lowered his voice. 'I want to visit my mother and not find her with an inch of make-up over obviously swollen eyes. I want my father's attention back on MooreCo and not constantly fixated on the past while important deals wither. I want him to stop finding excuses to invite *her* shadow along to every little thing.'

It hurt being nothing more than her mother's shadow in Aiden's eyes. Tash tipped her head—would he accuse her of copying another of his father's traits?—and regarded him. 'I think you would have preferred it if your father and I *were* having an affair.'

'Bloody oath I would. At least it would only be physical.'

Her blood was simmering well and truly now. But it was an ice-cold bubbling. She stood straighter. 'And why's that?'

'Because of who you both are: the CEO and the artisan. At least then there'd be no emotional threat.'

He said 'artisan' as if he meant 'courtesan'. Old scabs of worth tore open deep down inside. 'You don't think a CEO and a glass-blower could make it work?'

His laugh was harsh. 'Do you?'

She shrugged. 'I don't see why not. You certainly seemed interested enough.'

And suddenly she realised they weren't talking about Nathaniel at all. This was about those heavenly moments in the coatroom. When nothing but the chemistry between them mattered.

'I'm not talking short-term.' His eyes raked her from the ground up. 'That's totally possible. I'm talking more permanent.'

Emotional threat, he'd said. As though long-term relationships were pure danger to him. She picked her words with precision. 'Are you saying I'm unworthy of more?'

'Not at all. You're a beautiful woman, exceptionally talented. You're worthy of much more than you've had. But we come from completely different worlds.'

Thank you, Mr Darcy. 'I'm perfectly capable of running in your world. I did it for a year.'

'Jardine's world is small fry compared to the sharks I swim with.'

How apt.

'You wouldn't last a week,' he went on.

She straightened. 'Is that so?'

'Very much so.'

'Prove it.'

His eyes narrowed. 'I don't have to prove it. I know it.'

'Come on, Moore. Put your money where your mouth is.'

'You want to bet on it?'

Why not? 'Yes.'

'On whether or not you can survive in my world?'

'Yes. Because you have some fairly unattractive ideas about life and I think you're wrong.' Suddenly, proving him wrong felt vitally important. Both for his sake and hers.

'That's ludicrous.'

'You don't want me out of circulation?' she challenged and his eyes narrowed. 'I can't be distracting your father if I'm out with you all the time, can I? Isn't that what you want?' An opportunity for him to refocus on his wife.

Her words soaked into his busy brain as she studied him closely. Because yes, that was exactly what he wanted. Which would explain why he'd said yes, but why had she suggested it?

He leaned his hip onto the balustrade of the viewing window and crossed one foot carelessly over the other. 'What are you offering?'

'Not what you're thinking.' She shut that one down quick smart. 'Let me prove to you that status has no bearing on whether two people can get along.'

'Get along? Is that what we're talking about?'

She ignored him. 'On one condition.'

'This whole thing is your condition.'

'You extend me the same courtesy.'

Blue eyes narrowed. 'How?'

'You come to a few things with me.'

'What sort of things?'

'I don't know. I haven't thought of them yet. *My* things.'

'And this will prove what, exactly?'

'That you're a decent guy. And that relationships work both ways.'

He leaned in and murmured, 'And why is that important?'

Absolutely no idea. It just was. As important as proving she was up to mingling with the beautiful people. She was desperate to get a glimpse of the Aiden his father saw. The Aiden of youth.

If that Aiden even existed any more.

His lips parted in a knowing smile. He glanced inside where some of MooreCo's biggest clients were doing a great job of draining the bar and stripping the platters of shell-fish. 'If this is an example of how you handle an upper-class crowd—hiding out in the viewing room—then we're not off to a great start.'

'Forgive me for thinking I was invited to watch the foot-ball.' Tash tossed back her hair and straightened, indignation roiling through her. 'Let the games begin, then.'

With that, she strode to the door, opened it wide and marched through, a bright smile fixed on her face. 'Gentle-men...'

It took a special talent to be able to distract a group of over-privileged executives from an open bar and seafood buffet but Aiden took peculiar pleasure in watching Tash pull it off. He'd seen her work her magic at the launch party but that was a very different environment. This was the MooreCo corporate box—a much-lauded haven of excess and indulgence. A *what-happens-in-the-corporate-box-stays-in-the-corporate-box* type of place. A woman that looked like Tash was just as likely to find herself with a fifty tucked in her cleavage in this room.

But no...

She had them eating out of her hand.

Not that there wasn't an obligatory amount of speculation in all their eyes, but they weren't voicing it. And they weren't acting on it. They were being...respectful. That didn't happen all that often in here. Though a lot of business definitely got done here. Which was kind of the point.

'Are you just going to watch?'

The colour in her cheeks was high as she drifted towards him. And incredibly appealing. 'Looks like you're doing fine all by yourself,' he said, forcing away thoughts of how he could get her just as flushed. It involved kicking everyone else out of here and Tash pressing outwards against the big glass wall that separated them from the screaming fans.

He cleared his throat. 'What are you talking about with them?'

'The match. The installation. How glass-blowing works.'

'What happens when you've used all those up?'

'Then I fake interest in their business.'

A laugh barked out of him. 'Is that what you did with me? When you were asking questions about MooreCo?'

'You love talking about yourself, and your work by extension. It was the natural in.'

He couldn't help the chuckle. It was true. A robust ego was essential at his level of business.

She tipped her head in that way that was so like his father. 'No one's ever called you on that before?'

'Most people are too polite to actually comment.'

'Advantage of being an *artisan*,' she tossed back at him, popping a carrot stick between those full lips and then crunching down on it. 'Socially inappropriate is tolerated.'

He glanced at his father, deep in discussion on the far side of the room.

'Looks like he's not so distracted, after all,' she murmured.

'About time,' he muttered.

She kicked her chin up. 'Don't tell me you're not up to running things for a bit?'

'Oh, I'm up to it. I'd just like it to be on different terms.'

One brow lifted. 'Your terms?'

He stared at her. 'Different terms.'

She wasn't convinced. But she also wasn't going to press. 'So what do you think? Am I assimilating nicely?'

He couldn't help the smile. 'You're doing great.'

'Ready to eat your words, yet?'

'Not even close.'

'This room is full of ambitious executives. What more will it take to convince you?'

'A room full of their ambitious wives.' He knew the type well. Hungry for the success of their husbands and the life-style that it bought. Protective of whatever edge they had. Suspicious of beautiful young women trying too hard.

His mother in multiple guises, in other words. 'I'll review after that,' he finished.

'After what?'

'After you come with me to dinner Friday night. At Maxima.'

Dropping the name of the city's most exclusive restaurant did little more than thud mutely on the expensive carpet in the corporate box. It certainly didn't impress Tash. At all.

Her eyes narrowed. 'A business dinner this weekend. How convenient.'

'I have one just about every weekend.' Sometimes two. And why was he defending himself?

She scrunched her nose. 'How tiresome.'

Yeah, it was sometimes. Increasingly so. 'It's business.'

She leaned closer to him. Just a hint. 'And are you always about business?'

From anyone else he'd take that as a come-on. 'MooreCo's not going to run itself.'

'But what about fun? What about pleasure?'

He lowered his face and his voice. 'Are you offering?'

She let that one go through to the keeper. 'Can you even remember what fun felt like?'

God, she was fearless. 'I have a very good imagination.'

The tart smile she threw him should not have been such a turn-on. But it was. The women he dated were either amenable or aggressive. Great socially or under the covers but never both. The kind of forceful he liked in the bedroom didn't fly too well at gatherings like this. And the obliging, easy-going ones tended to be that way about sex, too.

What he wouldn't give for a woman who struck a reliable, happy medium. Confident socially. Confident in bed. Confident at business. Confident about themselves. The image of Tash all trussed up in her glass-blowing gear—and then just all trussed up—blazed into his mind.

'Aiden?'

He forced himself back into the conversation. The echo of her words reached his eardrum. 'Tomorrow? Working. What else would I be doing on a Monday?'

She let his inattention go, and it pleased him on some unwanted level that she didn't pout or make a big deal out of it. 'Silly question, I guess. Can you make any time in your day?'

'What for.'

'A road trip.'

That didn't sound like *some* time. That sounded like a lot of time. 'Where to?'

'I schmoozed your room. Now it's payback time.'

'Payback?'

'A glimpse into how the other half live. Tomorrow is half-price day at the underwater observatory.'

He blinked at her. 'No. Tomorrow is a work day.'

'You work every day.'

She had a point. But he wasn't about to ditch MooreCo to go sightseeing. He'd only just got his father back on task. The echo of Jardine's *insidious* crossed his mind. 'How about we go on the weekend and I'll shout you the ticket price?'

'That would be flagrant condescension.'

This had all the hallmarks of a set-up, but damned if he was going to let her think he wasn't up to it. He could work while he played thanks to the smartphone in his pocket. 'All right. Half-priced aquarium it is.'

'Underwater observatory.'

'Whatever.'

'No. An aquarium is perfectly lit and artificially stocked. What we'll be looking at is nature as it happens. You never know what you're going to see.'

He knew he was going to see her, and that was all that mattered. And that was a vaguely disquieting thought. He hadn't blown off work for a woman for a decade. If you didn't count a hot-and-heavy interlude with a catwalk model a few years back, and that had been so brief he'd barely been missed at the office.

But he'd sure got a lot of work done that afternoon. Sex always energised him. No matter how much he put into it. Not that anything physical was on the agenda for tomorrow; this was purely a psychological exercise. One good mind against another.

Weirdly, just as stimulating.

Though he wouldn't be hitting the office pumped up and ready to take on the world, afterwards. More was the pity.

'Better make it after lunch.'

CHAPTER SIX

SERIOUSLY? ALL THAT beauty out there and he was going to stare at his phone the whole time.

'I can see you,' Tash murmured. 'In the windows.'

Aiden lifted his eyes after a short pause, just long enough to finish reading his latest email. Glass panels surrounded them, keeping them dry and alive in this 360-degree submarine observatory. Curious fish bobbed around them, occasionally nosing the glass as if trying to work out why they couldn't cross into the human world.

'You're working,' he pointed out. 'Why can't I?'

'Because the whole point of this is to show me that you can take as good as you give. I was hoping your competitive spirit would have kicked in by now.'

He glanced compulsively back down at his phone and didn't quite catch himself in time.

'How many deals have you negotiated since we got to the observatory?'

The look he gave her would have made a lesser woman quail. 'I don't negotiate deals by email...'

'But?'

A long breath huffed out of him. 'But I've approved three.'

'Your guests are going to be so bemused when I come to dinner on Friday night and sit in the corner sketching.'

'It's not the same.' He smiled.

'It's exactly the same.'

He regarded her and then switched his phone off. 'Satisfied?'

'Not until it's in your pocket.'

He actually hesitated.

'Seriously, Aiden…' Tash laughed. 'I would have thought half a day's wait for your attention would keep your clients on their toes. Isn't that straight from your playbook?'

'It's not about them.'

'What's it about?'

He shrugged. 'Managing my workload.'

She turned back to her sketching very purposefully. 'Mmm-hmm.'

He fidgeted slightly in her peripheral vision. God, she loved silence. All the more because it was one of his favourite tools.

'Okay, Ms Corporate Coach, what do you think it's about?'

She flattened her pencil on her sketchpad and turned back to him. Since he'd asked so nicely. 'I think it's about controlling, not managing.'

'Not the first time I've been called a control freak.'

'There's nothing freaky about it. I'm sure it's very necessary in your role. But surely part of the skill of wielding control effectively is to stop it controlling you.'

He turned and stared at her. She ignored him and went back to her sketching. 'You're twitching to turn your phone back on right now,' she murmured under her breath. 'Admit it.'

The heat of his regard burned into the side of her tilted face. But then he simply swapped his phone to his left hand and held it out to her. It was impossible not to smile, yet it was only half smugness. The other half was genuine pleasure that he'd seen the truth of her words and not made an issue out of it.

She took the phone from him, slid it straight into her hand-bag and quietly went back to her sketching.

He stood. Paced up to the glass. Turned and looked at the whole space. Made much of examining the engineering. Then finally he returned to the comfortable leather bench by her side.

'Now what are you doing?' she asked.

'If I can't work I'll watch you work.'

Hmm. That's not distracting at all. She stabbed her pencil in the direction of all the water. 'Watch the fish.'

'I am watching the fish,' he said, not taking his eyes off what her fingers were doing. 'I'm seeing them as you see them.'

'I'm pretty sure we see them the same way.'

'Our eyes might but our brains don't.'

She turned away from her sketching. 'What do you see?'

He looked out to the dozens of grey bodies drifting around the observatory, then back at her occasionally flashing with silver from the sunlight far above. 'Lunch.'

Tsk. 'Heathen. Wait just a few more minutes; this thing happens on the half-hour...'

'What thing?'

She found his eyes. He really was bad with delayed grati-fication. Well, she wasn't about to enable him. 'A surprise thing. A delightful thing.'

'Delightful? What are you—Mary Poppins?'

'I enjoy nice things.'

He snorted. 'All women like nice things.'

'Nice *moments*. I'm not that fussed by possessions.'

'You grabbed my two-hundred-and-fifty-dollar smart-phone with quite a bit of glee just now.'

She turned to him. 'Aiden, if this is genuinely difficult for you I will happily give you your phone back.'

Really, what could he say without looking pathetic? Or desperate. Nothing at all.

'Nah. I'm good.'

The smile wouldn't be denied. 'Excellent,' she said through it. 'Give it a chance. If the sea life isn't spectacular enough for you now...'

Sure enough, the lights around them started to dim until the whole space was lit only by the fluorescence of the emergency exit sign to their far left. The natural light streaming down from the ocean's surface far above formed an eerie shaft of brilliance in the dark of the water. Then, as a slow reveal, a series of black lights mounted to the entire outer of the spherical observation bubble glowed into life, illuminating everything in the immediate surround in ultra-violet.

Those same drab, dark grey fish suddenly morphed into new creatures. One deep purple, one a deep blue, another almost crimson. Glittering, sparkling. All against the deep teal of the UV-lit depths.

Aiden caught his breath.

'Amazing, huh?'

'It's beautiful,' he whispered into the darkness and it was more intimate than if they were alone together in a bedroom. 'Is this how they see each other?'

'I like to think so. Who else is it for if not each other?'

She felt the exact moment that he turned to look at her. 'Is that how you see them?'

'I always see the potential before the actual.' Did space itself shrink under black light? Her tight breath certainly thought so.

'Some people might call that fanciful.'

'Some might. But there's a hidden side to the dourest creature. You just have to catch it in the right light.'

His gaze fell on a starfish, clinging to one of the pylons that held the jetty above them up off the ocean floor. Moments ago, he'd not even noticed it, she'd wager. But under new light, it was a rich orange rather than a dull brown to match the crusted timber of the pylon.

'Is that what you were drawing? There on the left?'

The left side of her notepad was filled with little sucker feet. She returned to one to give it some imaginary detail in the ethereal light. 'I'm going through a foot phase. Last time I visited, he was climbing the glass. I think I stayed for about six hours. Until he eventually moved on.' Every edge, every crease, every subtle shift of weight in those super-glue suckers. Imagining the whole time how it was going to translate in glass.

They fell to silence and Aiden stood and roamed quietly around the observation bubble that was empty of anyone but them. The more he looked, the more he saw and his curiosity gave Tash minutes of silence until, eventually, the automatic timer dimmed the external UV and raised the interior lights back to a dim glow. Back to reality.

She sighed.

'Why wouldn't they leave that on the whole time?' Aiden murmured, returning to her side.

'Because then it wouldn't be special. People might think that's what it really looked like below the surface. I like to imagine their world as vibrant and brilliant rather than dull and grey, but I know that the vibrancy is not for me.'

'So why confuse us with two different perceptions?'

'It's so spectacular their way. I think it's healthy for us to know there's a whole part of the spectrum that we don't experience. Keeps us humble.'

'Is that what you try to create? In your artwork?'

Was it? She did tend to see things in an extrasensory way while being creative. And she tried to portray that in her work. 'I don't have a problem with perceiving something differently in different environments. So maybe my work does the same thing, yes.'

She'd never thought of it that way before. Were her pieces doing for people what the black light did down here?

'Are we still talking about fish?'

Her eyes lifted to his. 'People too. Humans are particularly context-dependent.'

'How do you perceive me?'

Her snort ricocheted around the little glass room.

'Let me rephrase,' he modified on a glare. 'How do you perceive me differently in different contexts?'

She made him wait while she pretended to think about it. But she'd had her fill of thinking about Aiden so the comments came very naturally. 'In your professional context you're arrogant and decisive, impatient. Brilliant, of course, but with a tendency towards ruthlessness if there's something you want.' He didn't look entirely displeased by that description, which she perhaps should have anticipated. 'Socially you're good value, and a good contributor. You're generous with your money and time and mostly at ease—'

'You haven't seen me at Maxima yet.'

'That's more work than social. Anything there will be strategic.'

He gave her that point.

'Around your mother you're protective, tense, yet about as vulnerable as I've ever seen you. And around your father you're very much the son: respectful but frustrated.'

'Frustrated?'

'Like you just want him to get the heck out of the way so you can run MooreCo.'

He frowned at that. 'That's not how I feel.'

'Your body language says otherwise.'

'I love my father.'

'I believe you.' But then she'd yet to see him in a truly social situation with his dad. Their meetings to date were loaded with subtext. Until today. 'The two aren't mutually exclusive.'

He stepped closer. 'What about when I'm with you?'

'Like I said, you're good value—'

'Not socially. With *you*. When we're alone.' He leaned in as a young child sounded on the steps high above them. 'How do you perceive me now?' he murmured.

'Like a shark.' She blurted the first thing that came to her. 'Circling. Assessing. Flashing those teeth just enough to remind me they're there. Never taking your eyes off me. Relentless. Every move strategically planned.'

He gave her a grin full of those teeth now. 'Yet, you're not swimming away.'

'Sharks are as exciting as they are scary,' she breathed. 'All that danger. All that power and promise. Is he or isn't he all bluff?'

His lips hovered just a breath from hers. 'He definitely isn't.'

'You're very confident,' she murmured.

That gave him pause. 'Why do I get the sense that's not the word you wanted to use? You don't like confidence?'

'I do. Very much. But I don't automatically trust it.'

'Explain.'

'Confidence is captivating when it's earned. But it's exhausting when it's fabricated.' Kyle's was all bluster as it turned out. When the chips were down—when it mattered—he quailed. And a blusterer abhorred assurance in others.

Or maybe it was just in her.

Aiden's grin turned Cheshire. 'You don't think my confidence is justified?'

'It could all be for show.' But it wasn't. She knew it.

'Like yours, you mean?'

'You think I lack confidence?'

'Don't you?'

She considered her next move for a moment. 'Actually, I'm tempering it.'

That wiped the polished veneer off his gaze for the first time all day and Tash got the sense that he was really *seeing* her for a moment. 'Why?'

But that was a story she couldn't half tell. So best not to start. 'Not everyone likes self-assurance in practice as much as in principle.'

'Men, you mean?'

She wasn't about to answer that.

'So you just…what? Turn it off?'

'Down moderate it.' Her father had taught her, cruelly, the value he placed on modesty and her inability to contain it infuriated him. So she'd had to learn fast.

He grunted. 'I spend my days moderating. Maybe we're more alike than I suspected.'

'I thought I reminded you of your father.'

'Him too. You sure you're not a changeling stolen from my family?'

A ripple of gooseflesh ran down her back like an undersea tremor but she was saved from commenting by the arrival of a young mother and the toddler they'd heard earlier at the bottom of the spiral stairs.

Aiden withdrew with obvious regret, saying, 'Are you done with your drawings?'

'You trying to get me alone?' she murmured, totally on board with that plan.

He slipped his hand around hers—all warm and promising—and hauled her to her feet. 'I want to get you somewhere you can let all that confidence off the leash.'

'So, not entirely misplaced, then.' Aiden gasped, flopping onto his back next to her, chest heaving and skin damp. 'All that confidence.'

Tash turned her head to face him—the only part of her capable of movement after such an intense workout.

'You're a strange man, Aiden Moore.'

'Because I like paddle boats?'

Tash plucked her sea-soaked trousers away from her bent legs. She'd had to wade out to her hire-a-boat. 'Because you chose paddle boats as your duel weapon.'

'I used to come here on family holidays and race my cousins. It's a tradition in my family.'

Her heart did a tiny flip-flop at the thought of being considered part of his family. But that was dangerous thinking. 'Huh. So you stacked the deck.'

'Totally. I had to cover my butt in case you were the paddle queen of the West.'

'I *was* the paddle queen of the West.'

'I still won.'

'Your boat didn't have a hole in it. And your legs are like tree trunks.'

They went over it one more pointless time, how only a poor worker blamed her tools. And, again, the argument ended in laughter.

'Thank you for taking my phone,' he said, sobering, staring up at the two puffy clouds populating the blue sky.

She let her head flop sideways on the earth, towards him. He was lying much closer to her than she'd realised. 'You're welcome. How are you doing without it?'

'Better than I've felt in ages.'

That momentary flash of vulnerability deserved a reward. 'Well, thank *you* for the paddle-boat race. It's nice being able to give something one hundred per cent.'

'Yet you still lost.'

'Barely.' She reached over and thumped him, aiming for his stomach but encountering only hard, trained muscle under wet shirt. It felt as good as it looked.

Sigh.

'Seriously,' he said, 'why would you not give it your full effort, ordinarily?'

There was no judgement there, just curiosity. 'People don't like being shown up, as a rule.'

His groan was more of a curse. 'Do you know how long it's been since someone gave me a run for my money in any capacity? Bring it on.'

'Maybe no one wants to cross the rich guy?'

'You cross me daily.'

'I don't care about the money. Or the power. Or the sexy, expensive suits. But other people do. Maybe your cousins just *let you win* at paddle boats when you were young.'

His gasp turned into a chuckle. 'Wash your mouth out.'

The nearby water lapped the shore and washed against their beached paddle boats in dull *whumps* that exactly matched the steady thrum of her blood.

'Was it your father that taught you to downplay your assets?'

Every part of her tensed up. So much for the relaxation of the afternoon.

Aiden pressed, ignoring her flashing neon body language. 'I know it wasn't your mother. Not from the way you've spoken of her. Or was it Jardine?'

Pfft. 'I wouldn't give Kyle the satisfaction.'

He leaned up on one elbow and held her eyes. 'So your father, then.'

Trust didn't just materialise. It took risk. 'When I was seven I started to express my independence, like all kids.' His steady gaze was encouraging. 'Dad found it amusing for about five minutes.'

Aiden frowned. 'He punished you for testing the boundaries?'

'I think he punished me for being too much like her.'

The words bubbled up from her subconscious for the first time. 'He thrashed me a few times but realised pretty quick it wasn't effective. It just made me more determined to stand my ground. And that just inflamed him more.' She took a breath. 'We lived pretty much in a permanent state of conflict, the two of us, and he disciplined me with whatever he could without getting arrested by the Child Protection Authority: denying me permission for school excursions, withholding pocket money, refusing to sign my school notes so I'd get in trouble.'

Yeah, Eric Sinclair loved other people to do his dirty work.

'So what changed? If you were seven that was right before...'

'He found my off switch.'

Aiden frowned. And he hesitated for an age before risking, 'What was it?'

She picked at the grass on the bank of the shore. 'Mum. When I was bad, he hurt her instead of me.'

Blue eyes widened and flooded first with relief—that her father hadn't touched her, presumably—but then the reality of Eric's insidiousness dawned on him and they filled with the same expression she'd seen on his face when he'd locked them in the coatroom. Fury.

'Pretty soon he was hurting her preventatively, if he even got a whiff of attitude from me. It was like negative conditioning.'

Aiden just stared, unable to make words.

'As long as I was subservient and respectful and didn't show off or try to antagonise him, he left her alone. But if he got the slightest suggestion I was defying him...' She twisted her fingers around in the grass and pulled a dirt-packed clump free. 'It was quite effective.'

Aiden gently unfolded her fingers and let the dirt fall free, then wrapped them in his own warm strong ones. 'What changed?'

'She told me much later she'd spent all year trying to fig-ure out what she was doing to cause his rages. But she knew me, she saw me dying inside and she started watching him. Finally she realised what was happening.' Tash lifted her eyes. 'And so she called your father.'

Aiden froze. 'That's why they got back in touch after all that time?'

'He was the only one she knew could help.'

It took three swallows before he could speak clearly. 'And did he?'

She shuddered in a breath, glad to be rid of those days. 'Within a month we were in our own place and my father's hand was forced by how public it all was. Saving face was everything to him. He let her go. But not before trashing her name with everyone we knew.'

His eyes blazed. 'Did they even sleep together at all? Or did he just want your father to think that?'

The question was clear. *Did he destroy my family to save yours?*

'In her diary she talks about how ashamed she was to lie with him given the marks of abuse on her body, how all she could remember was how he used to look at her when she was young and beautiful.' She squeezed the fingers still curled around hers. 'But he made her feel beautiful one last time.'

Aiden frowned.

'As soon as he'd set the wheels in motion he went back to your mother. To you. I think he might have paid my father a visit, too. Warned him off.'

He fell to silence, and she let him process. As he did she poked around in her heart for the usual shame she felt when she thought about those awful days, but there was nothing there. As if revealing it had allowed it to flutter free. Adele

Sinclair had spent the next decade trying to undo the damage her husband had done, trying to patch up Tash's fractured little soul. Yet she was thirty before she realised none of those days were really about *her* at all.

He hurt her mother to punish Tash.

And he punished Tash because that hurt her mother much more than any bruises ever would.

Win-win.

Aiden's words came after a very long time. 'Do you hate him?'

'I will never love him. Or like him. But reading her diaries has helped me understand him. He was so weak. Such a victim. Even back at uni. I was the only one he could dominate.'

'And then you started showing your natural strength.'

'I didn't always feel strong.'

He sat up, taking both her hands in his. 'Never dumb yourself down, Tash. Not for anyone.'

She could have kept it light. Put them back on more familiar footing. 'Sometimes it's just easier.'

He nodded. 'Correction, then. Promise me you'll never dumb yourself down for me.'

He said that just as if they'd be spending a lot of time together. But the echo of such a serious statement—such a serious conversation—hung awkwardly between them. Until Aiden threw out a life preserver.

'So…what did you think I dragged you out of the observatory for, if not a lusty bout of paddle-boating?'

She grabbed the subject-change willingly. 'Something a whole lot less public.' But every bit as lusty.

'You came very willingly.'

There was a hot question in his gaze. A question she wasn't in a position to answer. 'There was a child there. I thought it would be more appropriate to move the conversation—' and the undercurrent '—elsewhere.'

He matched her smile. 'Good call.'

'Sadly, now we're exhausted.'

'I rally very quickly,' he assured her, leaning closer.

Oh, that she could believe. 'I promised your assistant I'd have you back at your office by four p.m. All those messages, remember?'

'Screw that. Simone will reschedule. I can even put on one of my *sexy* suits for you.' The ridiculous eyebrow waggle mended one of the fissures in her heart. Inexplicably.

Her laugh flung up high, then settled softly back down where they lay like a gossamer parachute. 'My work ethic is sound even if you're embracing your new phone-free status. I have a prototype piece to start work on tonight.'

The teasing dropped immediately and his eyes grew keen. 'The starfish?'

'Yes. I'm determined to capture those little tube feet just right.'

'Maybe not everything can be recreated in glass?'

She pulled herself up to a sitting position. 'Now it's your turn to wash out your mouth.'

He didn't want to let her go. It was evident in the deep blue depths of his eyes. But he pulled himself into a sit and smiled sadly. 'I have a favour to ask.'

'Wow. One lusty bout of paddle-boat racing and you think you can ask favours.'

'I want to watch.'

Everything in Tash's chest tightened up with a twisted kind of anticipation. But experience had taught her not to assume. 'Care to rephrase?'

'Your work. I want to watch you make the starfish.'

That was even more personal than what she'd thought he meant. Momentary panic robbed her of brain cells. 'Why?'

'I want to see the whole process.'

Again... 'Why?'

'Because it's interesting. And because it's your work.'

A small fist formed high in her gut, where her throat started. 'I usually don't work with an audience....'

Intent blue locked on her. 'Would you make an exception?'

The only person she'd ever blown glass for was her mother. It was something special between them, so that she could understand her daughter's passion. Maybe that was all Aiden wanted, too. She took a deep breath.

'Sure.' Though the permission was nowhere near as casual as that. 'It'll only be a test piece. I'll have to spend some time on it to get it right.'

'Test piece is fine.'

She narrowed her eyes as something dawned on her. He looked as awkward as she felt. 'You look very uncomfortable.'

'I don't do supplication.'

Her laugh exploded out. 'No. I can see that. How does it feel?'

He took his time answering, and then a word formed after his chest rose and fell heavily, just once. 'Odd.'

'Well, that's okay, then. As long as you realise how special this opportunity is.'

'Oh, I'm getting that loud and clear.'

Was he talking about more than just a glass-blowing demonstration? It was tempting to imagine.

'Thursday?' Because, secretly, there was no way she was letting him see her first feeble efforts. If she pushed herself, she could get somewhat proficient with the sea star by Thursday.

Preserving her dignity had become strangely meaningful around Aiden.

'See you then.'

CHAPTER SEVEN

A CHANGELING STOLEN from our family...

Aiden's words swirled around and through the troubling undercurrent from his father's startling pronouncement just days before. That he and her mother had been together at university. The moment he'd uttered the casual words in the observatory this afternoon, something had shifted and clicked in her subconscious. Like the barrels of a lock clunking into place.

Tash stared at the books scattered around her on the pretty rug on her lounge room floor. Yet there was nothing about it in her mother's diaries. Nathaniel suggested that was born of fear. It made sense. Adele Sinclair had feared many things about her husband; he absolutely was the sort to violate her most private thoughts in feeding his own ravenous paranoia. That would have been the lesser of many, many evils.

She shook her head and murmured, 'Why did you stay with him so long, Mum?'

Because she had made her bed, probably. Or maybe because she didn't think she would do better after she'd watched the love of her life walk away with someone else. From her mother's diaries it was clear that Eric Sinclair was no prize in their youth—never quite as bright, quick-witted or vibrant as the rest of their group of friends—but he'd apparently seemed harmless enough...then. In the years after they all went their separate ways his true colours emerged—or maybe they were drawn out of him by his fear and suspicion—and perhaps her mother stayed with him out of a deep-seated belief that she'd somehow *earned* her lot. Eric had resisted every subtle attempt his wife had made to change the dynamic in their relationship and he'd flat out refused her attempts to seek counselling and her threats to leave to *force* things to be better.

His irrational fear made so much more sense if Nathaniel and Adele had actually been sleeping together.

Tash reached for the palest of the diaries. The oldest. She'd pored over these multiple times; she knew what was there. Or not there. She knew there was no mention of any kind of intimacy between her mother and Nathaniel in their university days, but maybe she was missing something. Something between the lines.

Or between the pages....

She left blank pages in the diary where I would be, Nathaniel had said.

She flicked through the earliest pages in the book. Tales of going to the movies with Laura, or class with Eric, or lunch at the student cafeteria with Nathaniel. But nothing more meaningful. A few pages wailing about some tough exams and—

There!

A blank page. After her first-year exams. Positioned so it just looked like the passing of time. And *there*—another. On a mid-semester break early in second year to a sleepy little town with Laura. At least it had appeared to be just the two of them, but there was a gently humorous tale of her and Laura in the back seat of the car killing time with a word game.

So if Laura was in the back seat with Adele, who was driving?

No mention. Just another blank page two days into their trip. *Did* Nathaniel occupy the blank pages of her mother's diaries just as he'd said? And if he did, what was she being so careful to leave out? He wasn't completely absent; Tash supposed that would have been as telling as full disclosure when Eric knew the group of friends spent so much time together. So what had they done that warranted blank pages?

It wasn't hard to guess.

Her mother and Nathaniel had been lovers. Years before that *one time.* And then something pulled them apart long enough for Laura to get her hooks into the man she, apparently, had a thing for all along and she got pregnant by Nathaniel.

He and her mother had reunited, according to Nathaniel, but when he'd discovered Laura was pregnant with his child, he'd made the hard choice and stuck by the woman he didn't love.

Which left Eric the last single man standing. Conveniently poised to pick up the pieces of a shattered Adele. Lucky for Tash or she might not exist at this moment. She'd come along not long after Aiden had. Almost as if her mother couldn't bear to watch the man she loved be father to someone else's child when she was—

An icy chill worked its way through Tash's arteries.

She'd come along not long after Aiden had. And he'd come along pretty much straight away thanks to Laura and Nathaniel's irresponsible hook-up.

A flicker-show played out behind Tash's eyes. Of the tilt of Nathaniel's head when he laughed, so like her own. The two of them cheering the same football team on and her turning to smile into eyes the same colour as her own. Their similar taste in food and in humour. His obsessive focus on her and the way he was letting his business slide to spend time with her.

A changeling stolen from our family…

The chill turned to a thick, stagnant goo that made beating agony for Tash's straining heart.

What if there was a reason she and Nathaniel had connected so instantly? Were so alike? What if something other than heartbreak came of those few weeks that her mother and Nathaniel were back together? Before he discovered he was a father.

Her heart hammered. What if Adele was pregnant, too, when they broke up? That would explain why her mother would have stayed with a man like Eric. And it would explain why Tash had nothing in common with Eric Sinclair. And—absolutely—why he'd have hated her enough to treat her the way he did.

Because maybe he *wasn't* her real father. And maybe he knew it. And maybe the reason her daddy had hated her so much was because of whose genes she carried, not because of who *she* was.

Blind hope welled, warm and soothing through the thick dread. What if Nathaniel Moore was her real father? A man that she could respect. A man that she could love so very easily. A man worthy of the title. A raft of tingles settled through her body and it was almost the angelic touch of her mother from on high, soft and benevolent and comforting…

And all-confirming.

A slight tremble started up deep in her muscles. How different might her life have been if she'd had Nathaniel as a father instead of Eric? A father who encouraged and praised her successes rather than trying to break her. A father who moved heaven and earth to keep their family together instead of throwing it away in a poisonous, vengeful and public outburst.

She blinked back tears.

God, how much better might she have been being raised a Moore, like Aiden, instead of a—

The blue diary slipped from her suddenly nerveless fingers. *Like Aiden.*

If she was a Moore then that meant Aiden was—

Nausea swilled in and replaced the breathless excitement of moments before as she replayed the memory at the football game when Nathaniel had urged her, so intently, not to get involved with Aiden.

Promise me...

A sickening kind of dread took root deep in her soul. The longer she sat there, the more awfully, horribly right it felt. Her stomach muscles locked up hard on the implications.

Aiden was her half-brother.

There was no question about *his* heritage.

She was losing hours each day imagining herself with him, thinking about what it might be like to have him in her life on a more permanent basis.

But she'd cast him more as a lover than a—

Self-loathing, raw and all too familiar, washed through her and she battled the duelling desires. To be a Moore: Nathaniel Moore's daughter, to have a decent father finally, someone she could relate to and connect with. And respect.

But to be Aiden's *sister...*

All the saliva in her mouth decamped.

How could that possibly be? Surely her body would know, even if her mind didn't?

She saw herself twisted back in his arms amongst the expensive coats, his tongue challenging hers. She remembered the rush of excitement and expectation as he'd slipped strong arms around her. She heard herself flirting wildly, putting a toe into the waters of the sexual attraction that raged between them.

And she pressed her palm to her suddenly roiling belly.

Shame flooded through her, but she could live with that. Kyle had made her out to be little better than a tramp at the end of their relationship—over-sexed and under-barefooted—and

she'd managed to swallow the humiliation of that very public breakup and keep on surviving.

She could do it again. This time in private.

But rejecting Aiden now, after the promise she'd made
him this afternoon…. If she cancelled Thursday on him,
he'd demand an explanation. And rightly so. Except she just
wasn't free to explain. Nathaniel was out of the country this
week with Laura, trying hard to mitigate the damage he'd
caused—a very different thing from trying to save his marriage, Tash suspected—so she couldn't call and drop a grenade into that careful work.

So that meant she had two choices—cancel or go ahead
with the glass-blowing demo.

Could she keep him at bay for the time he was with her?
Heat and danger were her friends in the hot shop. It was work
for her; she could behave professionally. And he wasn't about
to force himself on her, right?

Surely, they could pass an hour in each other's company
without doing anything inappropriate.

Surely.

Aiden jogged down the old, paved, port road towards Tash's
studio. City council had established this part of town as an
arts precinct decades before, back when artists were the obvious choice to sequester away in substandard buildings. They
got tenants to keep an already seedy part of town from wors-
ening and they also got points for supporting the very vocal
art community.

Double win.

Maybe someone in council lacked foresight though, because you'd think they'd have put limited zoning on the wa-
terfront precinct in case the social dynamic ever changed and
they wanted to use the land for something else. It did change,
and now rich people were buying up the old wool stores and

converting them into creative, heritage-style accommodations left and right of the remaining artists. Squeezing them out incrementally. But the council couldn't evict the arty set without causing office-losing scandal.

Tash didn't lack foresight when she traded a pile of her best works for her quarter of the then derelict building. She had a great studio in what was fast becoming a great part of town. The artists and the wealthy mainly enjoyed a symbiotic relationship: the presence of the cashed-up residents made sure cafés and buses came to their part of town and that the precinct bustled even at night where it used to be a dark, port wasteland. And the artists loaned the area a whole bunch of cool-factor credibility.

'Knock-knock.'

Aiden paused at the last door in the row, a heavy sliding timber thing that flaked enough to tell anyone passing that it was occupied by an artist. In case the hot air pumping out of it wasn't clue enough.

Tash appeared in the opening a moment later, dressed in her usual glass-blowing gear—battered, closed-in boots, overalls and a T-shirt. Its sleeves were the only thing that was different from the first time he'd seen her all those weeks ago. That and the tiny leap of pleasure she failed to disguise before she got her expression under control and flooded it with caution.

Sigh. So they were back to caution. That didn't bode well.

'Sorry I'm late,' he said. Wouldn't it be great if that were the reason for her wary expression?

'I thought you might have changed your mind.'

Was that *hope* hiding behind her brown eyes? 'Are you kidding? After working so hard to get you to let me come along in the first place?'

It was easy to joke but it really wasn't all that funny. He was halfway through negotiations before he realised he didn't know *why* he wanted to come so badly. It wasn't just because he wanted to see the developing starfish—though that was what he'd told her. And it wasn't because he wanted to see her again—though he very much did after he realised it could otherwise be a whole working week before he saw her again.

The closest he could get to his own version of truth— from somewhere way down deep—was because it was the one thing she'd told him he couldn't have. Last time he'd stood here in her doorway. She'd seemed so shocked at the idea of revealing her craft. Her self. As if he'd asked her to strip naked and dance for him. And so it had intrigued him.

Actually, he thought she might have danced naked before she agreed to this.

And now he was imagining her naked. And she was staring at him as if he were deficient.

Awesome.

'Well, here you are,' she said, grudgingly. 'Do you want to see the MooreCo pieces?'

Not really—he just wanted to stand here with her a moment longer acting like a total sap. 'Sure. Lead on.'

She turned and he enjoyed the bonus view of her sexy hip-sway ahead of him. It helped force his mind back into more familiar, physical territory. He focused on the sensation.

'This is the shoal taking shape....'

Three dozen tiny, silver-stained fish hung suspended from the studio roof, cleverly bonded together with invisible glass welds so that as the biggest pieces changed direction in the light ocean breeze the whole shoal seemed to follow, with fishy, military precision.

He could well imagine them glinting and bouncing prisms around MooreCo's glass entry gallery. And their clients staring up at them from underneath. To replicate that view he crouched and examined the whole effect from below. Somehow, she'd managed to make looking at them from below feel like looking down at them from above. Like being under and above the water at once.

'It's extraordinary, Tash.' The compliment was out before he thought it through. He usually liked to reserve his hand a little longer. Until it counted.

Apparently not today.

'I'm contemplating another three dozen. It looks big here but they'll be lost in your foyer.'

'I can't wait to see it installed.'

She struggled to disguise her smile. On one hand, it pleased him to have pleased her, but it disappointed him that she didn't want to show him that. She wouldn't even give him a hint of her pleasure. He thought something had changed between them after the paddle-boating.

Or maybe this was the universe giving him an out. Because he really shouldn't be worried if a woman wasn't emotionally forthcoming. What the hell use were emotions to him?

'This is only the base element,' she continued. 'These are some of the hero pieces.…'

The more she showed him, the harder it was for her not to reveal her pretty pink glow at his praise. Pretty soon, making her blush was all he could focus on. She fought it—inexplicably—but she was losing.

And *that* was definitely familiar territory. He loved a well-fought battle…as long as it came with a resigned surrender at the end. And not on his part. It was much safer to focus on the tantalising tingles than on the other feelings bubbling away below the surface.

The ones whispering at him to come here today. In case bending her to his will in this way might be catching.

Because that spoke of a desperation he wasn't about to acknowledge.

She carried on with her impromptu tour of the glass pieces littering her studio.

He leaned on a workbench after they'd examined the final piece. 'This is really going to blow our clients away. They'll be late to our meetings because they're standing down in the foyer, lost in your undersea world.'

Again with the pleasure. Until she dipped her head.

Why did she keep fighting it? Why not just go with it?

Every other woman he'd known just went with it. Some faster than others, admittedly, but ultimately they acquiesced. Persistence. He'd been raised with it on two fronts. A father who believed that reward only came from effort, and a mother who'd taught him, through example, the value of dogged determination. Whenever there was something she wanted, she just stayed the course and remained unmoved and—usually—things ended up going her way. She worked on the principle that if you ignored 'no' often enough eventually it became 'yes'.

'So, has our lesson started?' he nudged, figuring that if the studio was going to be full of tense heat between them they might as well melt glass with it.

She looked him up and down. 'You're dressed okay.'

His wardrobe didn't have a lot of grunge in it but he'd managed to pull together an old-looking sweater, jeans and boots. She didn't need to know how much he'd paid to get that look in the first place.

'How come I have to have long sleeves when you don't?'

She lifted one critical brow. 'I've been doing this all my life. You're going to have sparks flying everywhere.'

'Doesn't that happen every time we get together?'

Her expression flattened. 'Hilarious. You want to learn or not?'

'Wow. Tough room.'

'I need to know you're concentrating before I let you near a vat of what is effectively molten lava.'

He forced his brows down. 'I'm listening. Honestly.'

She thrust a face shield at him and slid regular goggles on herself. 'This will stop your retinas from ulcerating,' she murmured, leading him to the kiln that pumped intense heat back at him. At the last minute, she also tossed him a pair of enormous fire-retardant gloves. 'And your skin from melting.'

'Is this really necessary?' he asked, feeling very much like a catcher in a baseball game.

She turned and glared at him. 'Do you want to watch or not?'

Did she seriously think that a few layers were going to protect her? He held the ridiculous gloves up either side of him and she continued.

Since he was a silver-lining kind of person he cheerfully told himself that the face shield might mean he couldn't smell her the way he wanted, but, in better news, it meant he could check her out without her knowing. He took full advantage of that as Tash slid the door open on the gaping maw of the furnace with hands covered in her own fire-retardant gloves. Then she turned to him.

'Pass me that blowpipe.' She nodded at a four-foot tube laid out on her workbench next to a medieval torture rack of tools. She took the pipe from him and raised it over her head, dipping it squarely into the middle of the orange glow within the furnace and turning it steadily, as if she were twisting up a forkful of spaghetti. After a hypnotic twist-a-thon, she backed up, withdrawing a blazing, deadly ball on the end of her pipe, turning, turning constantly. Her tanned shoulders flexed at the weight exchange as she lowered it down onto a waiting brace.

'The bolus is two thousand degrees,' she said, over the roar of the open furnace, turning it steadily. 'To make it into a vessel I have to introduce an air pocket inside. The air does part of the work. Right now my hand's job is just to keep the glass hot and moving.'

She did that, carefully and methodically. One hundred per cent focus. She squeezed a saturated sponge over the middle of the blow tube with her free hand, sending steam billowing up and around them both. It left a filmy sheen of moisture across her bare skin, droplets clinging to every hair on her body.

'That's so I can put my lips to the tube safely.'

Wait… 'You're going to suck that thing?'

She snorted. 'That's a fast way to kill yourself. No, I'm going to blow it. But I can't start until the shape is better.'

She reached for one of the torture-rack tools, a thick, burned wad of drenched newspaper. At least it once had been; it was mostly charcoal now. With nothing but her bare hands, she slapped the saturated newspaper to the underside of the molten mass and cupped it, shaping and polishing the glowing glass ball until he practically forgot she had newspaper in her hand at all. It was as if she were stroking the glass into compliance with her bare touch, persuading it to be what she wanted it to be. Massaging it with her courage and mastery.

His entire body responded, imaging her artist's hands polishing the shape of his muscles, massaging his flesh into compliance. Persuading him with her proficient touch.

He gritted his teeth against the sensation.

You just want what you can't have.

Damned right he did. But he wasn't a total creep. He wanted her to want him just as badly. She *couldn't* be totally indifferent to him, not when he was so very aware of her.

Could she?

He distracted himself with conversation. 'Don't you have better tools?'

'If you walked into a hot shop two millennia ago you'd see very similar tools. Sometimes the old ways are just the best.'

The shifting facets in the glowing, molten mass hypnotised him as she worked it around and around until it looked as if she were polishing a ball of toffee. Aiden stepped up hard behind her and laid a gloved hand on her shoulder so she knew he was there.

The blowpipe lurched as she fumbled a turn.

'What would happen if you didn't keep it moving?' he asked.

'Um...' She rounded her shoulders and got the momentum under control again. 'It would start losing form the moment the inertia stops.'

'Would it drop off?'

'Keep distracting me and we'll find out.'

She was right. Manipulating a kilo of volcanic eruption was not the time to be peppering her with questions. He stopped talking and concentrated on watching over the top of her head.

She twirled for a few minutes longer and then lifted the whole thing higher, pivoted it sideways onto on its brace and placed the end of the pipe to her lips. He didn't see her shoulders rise or her ample chest expanding with breath, but he saw the bolus expand a little. Just a little. Just enough.

Looked as if it was going to be a fat little sea star.

It was like watching a bagpipe player. Steady and controlled. And watching her lips working the end of the pipe so expertly gave him a personal heat that had nothing to do with the roasting warmth coming off the three furnaces in the room.

Pervert.

He forced his attention off Tash and onto the shape beginning to form on the end of the tube. She swung the whole thing sideways and onto a pair of braces with a seat in between them. With two thousand degrees practically sitting in her lap she kept the thing moving, horizontally, on the braces and started working with some of the tools. A cupped block that gave the blob a pear-shaped bottom—ah, his favourite shape—and a pair of nasty-looking pincers that trimmed and poked and shaped and cut as the whole thing endlessly spun.

Twirl, snip, twirl, snip. Every cut liberated more of the creature within the glass and she tapped the edges of each leg to open some space between them. They spread joyously outwards with the force of the spinning.

His body twitched again.

God, there was something so sexy about her proficiency. And her focus. And the sheen of sweat on her body amid the roasting heat swilling all around them. It made it near impossible to concentrate on what her hands were doing.

He moved behind her again and leaned down until his eyes were at the same level as hers. Conveniently, that meant curling his torso around her somewhat.

The turning and snipping faltered. 'What are you doing?' she choked, low and concerned, twisting towards him just slightly.

'I want your eye level. I want to see it how you see it.'

He wanted to *feel* what she was feeling—if he couldn't *be* felt. But the first thing he wanted was to not remain separate from her for a moment longer while this sensual display was going on.

'It's like there's actually a mental connection between you and the glass and your hands are just there to preserve the illusion.'

Her back cranked straighter and her shoulders set. 'You think I'm just willing the glass into shape?'

'Right now, I think you could talk it into doing anything just to please you.'

Tash stood violently and scooped the blowpipe and nascent starfish up with her, dislodging Aiden's clinging presence as she went. His words carried a payload of subtext and none of it was appropriate given what she knew.

Thought she knew.

But, oh, my God, if she was right…

She plunged the starfish back into the reheating drum to boost its temperature and to buy herself a few moments away from him. She was used to the furnace's scorching heat, but its extremes kept him safely back.

'Can you please pass me one of the glass straws on the work table?' she asked back over her shoulder. All business.

Colour—that was what this piece needed. And space—that was what *she* needed. Adding colour to the molten piece required lots of twisting and turning and Aiden simply couldn't stand that close while she did that or she'd take his eye out with the end of her pipe.

Tash pulled the starfish out of the drum and transferred the emerging shape onto a glass rod for easier handling, and then she fired up the blowtorch and took the orange colour stick from Aiden's waiting hands. She exaggerated every movement so that he wouldn't have an opportunity to step that close again.

Lord, bad enough having him here, in her studio, watching her work, without him bringing a whole lot of *tsss* into what was already a hot enough space. Just had to stay focused.

As he'd noted, she was very determined.

He watched her in silence as she dribbled melted colour along each leg under the sear of the brace-mounted torch repeatedly, until all five legs had organic colour streaking down them. She pulled the lot away from the torch and waited the few seconds for the glass to cool enough to see the natural colours emerging.

It was so hard not to glow as bright as the sea star at the awe in Aiden's gasp. 'Cool, huh?' she said. 'Furnace-born.'

Steadfastly ignoring his closeness, she set about adding dozens of blobs to the underside of each leg and then went over the lot again, pressing an indent into each little sucker. Not perfect yet, but she was getting there.

Aiden began circling her as she worked, watching from all angles. Wherever he moved, she felt his regard despite his mask; the intensity of his stare, every bit as scorching as the heat she worked with. He reminded her of the shark again....

Circling.

Waiting.

Finally, the sea star was finished. She killed the blowtorch and the sudden silence was startling. She dropped her goggles and Aiden flipped his visor up. As she laid the starfish on the edge of her brace its legs curled and sank in a slow, descending wave exactly like the real thing—as though it really were alive—until two legs hung over the edge of the brace as it would hang over a shelf. Or a fish tank. Or a bookcase.

Just like the one she'd watched at the observatory bending around the sharp angles of the timber pier.

It wasn't the best that she'd made, but it was the best she was going to do today. The intensity of Aiden's stare, the intimacy of him watching her work...if ending that came at the price of a half-arsed starfish, then so be it. She apologised to the spirit within the glass as she gloved it carefully into the kneeling oven where it would slowly cool over the next twenty-four hours to preserve the integrity of the glass. Then she slid the heavy door closed.

And her best excuse for not facing Aiden evaporated.

'Your arms must be screaming,' he murmured, coming closer now that all the heat was safely behind asbestos doors. At least the heat from the furnace. The friction between the two of them was still creating its own blazing warmth.

'They're used to it.' She backed away a step for each one he took towards her, busying herself with removing her gloves and setting her tools back to rights. 'It's my back where I tend to feel it.'

Idiot. She'd spoken just for something to say—surely, while they were talking she couldn't be busy thinking about anything else—but he took that as encouragement and crossed to her more quickly than she could avoid.

'Here,' he said, spinning her around and tossing his safety gloves. 'Let me do something about that.'

No. No, no, no… She tried to twist out from under his strong hands as they kneaded down into her aching muscles but they were too powerful. And warm. And way too good. How often had she wished for someone to do this at the end of a long day in the hot shop? Or even a short one. His fingers probed and kneaded the worst of the developing bunches, rhythmically pressing into her and then easing off again, using the same kind of rhythm that she seduced the glass with.

Seduced…

Tash twisted away without any hope of it being subtle. 'Aiden—'

He raised his hands beside his shoulders in as non-threatening a manner as a man of his size and presence could possibly achieve. 'Tash…' he mocked.

'This is not going to happen.' It just couldn't. And wouldn't.

'You're attracted to me.'

'I'm—' *So dead.* 'No, I'm not.'

'Liar.'

Yes, more than she'd ever lied in her life. He was making her into one. '*This*—' her finger ping-ponged between his chest and hers '—is not going to happen.'

'Why not?'

Frustration roared through her. At being put in this position. 'Because I don't want it.'

'Your body disagrees, it seems.' His eyes narrowed. 'What am I missing?'

She pressed her lips together. Anything she said could be used against her in the court of Aiden.

'Am I not good-looking enough for you? Not rich enough?'

She threw him a glare. 'I'm not interested in your money or how pretty you are.' She used the word intentionally to distract him from his line of questioning. 'Give me some credit.'

'I believe you. And that intrigues me. I've never met anyone who puts so little value on the things I have to offer.'

'I'm just a challenge to you. The novelty will wear off in no time.'

His eyes darkened. 'I wish that was true. Because I'd understand that.'

Her breath tripped over itself and backed up in her throat. 'What don't you understand?'

He stepped closer. 'This hold you have over me. I'm not in the habit of begging.'

'You haven't begged.'

'Feels like I have.'

'Why, because I didn't crumble at the first sexy smile?' Damn. She hadn't meant to admit that.

If nothing else, he was a gentleman—when it counted. He didn't call her on her slip. But the intensity in his gaze doubled. 'I'm intrigued by you. I respect you. I even admire you.'

He said the words like they were anathema. 'Are those not qualities you're accustomed to in your...dates?'

His stare grew bleak. 'Not particularly. But they have pretty faces. And great bodies. And they're very...sympathetic to my way of doing things.'

His eyes grazed her.

'Maybe it's that simple, then,' she murmured, scrabbling around for a legitimate answer that didn't mean betraying anyone's trust. 'You've grown spoiled. And bored. Perhaps you're just hungering for a challenge?'

Those blue eyes narrowed. And the step he took towards her officially pushed her up against the wall of her studio.

He placed a braced fist on either side of her. 'That would explain it.'

Her hands came up to rest on his chest and his eyes flicked down, full of speculation.

Until she pushed against him and all she could think about was how gorgeously hard his chest was. 'Unfortunately,' she said as she slid out from his imprisonment, 'I'm not all that sympathetic to your cause. Certainly not enough to oblige you.'

He shook his head. 'You will.'

The certainty made her bristle. 'Actually, I won't.'

'Why won't you?'

'Can't I just not want to?'

'If I thought you genuinely didn't want to I'd turn and walk out right now. You do want to.'

'You're very fond of telling me what I should be thinking.'

'I just think I know you better than you do.'

'No. You're just hearing what you want to hear.' She twisted away from him, picked up the still-hot blowpipe and wielded it across her chest. Like a weapon. 'Now, if you don't mind I have a lot of work to do today and I've already lost the morning catering to the whims of my commissioning client.'

His left eye twitched but he didn't argue.

'Fair enough. I'll leave you to it.' He pulled the open visor off his head. Sweaty hat-hair only made him look infuriatingly more handsome. 'But we'll resume this conversation tomorrow after Maxima.'

Oh, crap… *The dinner.*

A function she couldn't possibly attend anymore. Not knowing what she now knew. Not knowing how terrible at deterring his touches she was, how much her own body would sabotage her best intentions. How could she sit beside him as he slid those bedroom eyes her way and not feel what she didn't dare feel?

Or if he touched her.

Or—her stomach knotted—tried to kiss her again.

Based on the steam in his expression right now he would do those things unless she explained. But she couldn't explain; that was for his father to do.

By the way, Aiden, you have a half-sister and she's been working with us these past weeks. Oh, and—PS—you've had your tongue in her mouth.

Surprise!

If she cancelled, she'd need a rock-solid excuse or he'd see right through it. And if she went, then the night would be full of knowing glances, the two of them against the world. Sitting pressed together. Smiling. Being delightful.

Just she and her—

Even her mind choked on the word.

—brother.

CHAPTER EIGHT

'GET DRESSED.'

The first thing Tash thought when she opened her cottage door to find Aiden leaning there, all concerned and gorgeous, was how darned edible he looked in a dinner suit. The second thing she thought was what had happened to all her self-control—and her dignity—that she couldn't even last two seconds without feeling something she shouldn't.

'I'm *sick*, Aiden,' she overcompensated.

'You're a terrible liar.'

'I told you on the phone—'

'Yeah, I know you did. That way you could hide the fact that you're pink and healthy and the least sick person I've seen all week.'

'So someone tells you they're sick and your first reaction is to go to their house and give them grief?'

He held a translucent plastic bag high. It sagged with the weight of something inside. 'No. My first reaction is to go to their house with chicken broth.'

Tash stared. He'd brought her soup.

A whole bunch more feelings she'd promised herself not to allow came rushing to the fore. She almost wished she *were* sick so that she could accept kindness from him. Instead of tossing it back in his face with her lies, which she had to do.

She crossed her arms.

'Thank you, Aiden.' He glared.

'Oh, please. You just needed an excuse to check up on me.'

'I needed you to feel better.'

Even he looked surprised at the word that slipped across his lips. *Need.* Tash forced her resolve to hold. 'Uh-huh. And that's why the first words from your mouth were "get dressed"?'

'You opened the door looking so bloody gorgeous and *not sick.* That's why I told you to get dressed. Which I notice you still aren't doing.'

'That's because I'm not going with you to dinner.'

'Why not? You gave me your word.'

Lying just sat so uncomfortably on her. She was sure it showed. 'I don't feel well. What if I'm viral? I'll give it to everyone there.'

'Instead of just me.'

'Hey, you came knocking on *my* door, remember?'

'You don't sound much like a sick person, either.'

'What do you want? A temperature reading?' Nice one. Plant the idea. He was suspicious enough to pull out a thermometer, too.

His eyes narrowed and she could practically *see* the cogs turning in his sharp mind. 'Okay, I'll come in, then. A nice night in, behind closed doors. Just you and me.'

No. That was not an option. No matter how fantastic it sounded. Because if he came into her house there was no way soup would be the only thing steaming up the place. The arms wrapped around her torso tightened. The hug helped a little, even if it was her own. Her face must have spoken volumes.

'What's going on, Tash?' He leaned on her doorframe. 'I thought you were up for this.'

'That's a little direct, isn't it?' Even for him.

'I'm talking about dinner.'

'Oh. I just—' *Oh.* 'Why don't you just go yourself?' Away. As far from her as possible would be good.

'I am going, of course. But I wasn't expecting to be date-less.'

Was that his problem? A face-saving thing? 'I'm sure you have any number of women on standby for occasions just like this one.'

'Occasions where my present date is lying through her beautiful teeth?'

She wanted to be angry but how could she? She *was* lying. 'Can't I just ask you to trust me that I have a good reason not to go?'

His eyes roamed over her face and finally settled on her eyes, curious and probing. 'Is it the dinner or the after-dinner that has you all worked up?'

'Aren't they a package?'

'No. One is not conditional on the other.'

She narrowed her eyes. 'So we could just have dinner?'

Dinner was doable. Friends had dinner all the time. Siblings had dinner all the time, too.

'We can totally just have dinner. Is that what this is about?'

This is about me not trusting myself for five minutes in your company. But she could do dinner. Dinner was just eating and talking, right? And then he'd leave her alone. Their scoresheet would be square.

She spun away, towards her bedroom. 'Give me ten minutes.'

Aiden watched the light spring of Tash's steps and then closed the front door behind him and placed the pointless soup on the nearest flat surface. Then he yanked it up again and looked for something a bit sturdier, a bit less polished timber-y. His mother's meticulous upbringing coming to the fore. She wasn't much on mess.

He crossed to the kitchen bench and set the soup there.

Then he turned and looked around Tash's house, studying the hotchpotch of items pinned to her fridge door as he went. Bills, takeaway menus, a gorgeous photo of what could only be a younger Tash with a sparkly-eyed woman. Her mother.

Her little cottage was full of modest, mass-produced furniture that would have been bland if not for the liberal addition of throws and rugs and a disparate collection of bright wall-mounted artwork. There was no particular style or artist; it was just crazy. Like the woman herself—complex, contradictory.

Confusing.

Hadn't they been on the same page on Monday? On the same page and even in the same book, and he didn't often find someone who had the same book he did. He'd been as clear as he could be, and his heart—which didn't make a habit of speeding up for just anyone—had actually lurched when she'd smiled at him and followed him so eagerly out of the underwater observatory. She'd thought she knew what they were leaving for, and she'd been comfortable with what she thought.

He'd seen it.

Yet here she was baulking—and lying, though about as miserable an attempt as anyone he'd ever met—to get out of whatever obligation she felt about what was planned for après dinner.

He eyed the one old piece of furniture in the room, an overstuffed chair covered in an Aztec-patterned throw. That was more his size. He just about groaned as he sank down into its welcome comfort. It was a chair made for lounging in front of a game, or a long night of conversation or—he looked at the sturdy armrests—something else. All he needed was a glass of red and Tash and he was good for the evening.

Except that she'd looked almost panicked at the thought

of the two of them here alone. Ludicrous after what they'd virtually committed to earlier in the week, but there it was.

Maybe that was what was behind this fake illness.

Nerves.

Under normal circumstances, he wouldn't have had much time for indulging the modest blushes of his date, but this was different. This was Tash. He found himself prepared to indulge any of her quirks if it meant she'd let him near her. Let him touch her. So a few blushes were a no brainer. He'd pull back a little, reduce the haste and increase the flirt. Romance her. Women liked that. And Lord knew he savoured the agony of anticipation. It would make eventual success so much sweeter.

He'd once been described as 'relentless and persistent' in a protracted negotiation, but it was those qualities that eventually won the day. He literally outlasted and outgunned everyone else. The same qualities would help him now. He understood nerves—actually, he *didn't*, but he understood them in someone else—and he understood reticence. No one liked to surrender, especially not someone as spirited as Tash.

And that was pretty much what it was, wasn't it? Surrender.

He tuned in to the sounds of shuffling behind a half-closed door as Tash dressed for a dinner she didn't want to go to.

Relentless it was, then. And Tash would be his for the taking.

He almost—*almost*—regretted that. Because taken was taken and then what would sustain him if not the thrill of the chase? He knew himself well enough to know what to expect then.

Not a problem for tonight. Tonight was about the onset of the campaign.

Operation Romance.

CHAPTER NINE

HONESTLY, IF HE touched her one more time she was going to explode. And not in a good way.

Tash was certain that Aiden hadn't been this...hands-on... the other times he'd been with her, but it was hard to stay certain when every brush clouded her memory, every light pressure from those strong fingers muddled her mind. Or, worse, the times he *didn't* touch her, but came within infuriating millimetres and then all she could think about was whether he was going to make contact again.

Dreading that moment.

Wanting that moment.

It had taken her about twenty-five seconds behind her bedroom door to come up with a plan to get through the evening. A great mental filing system that would give her some way of managing the feelings that had started swilling through her blood as soon as she opened the door to see him leaning there, waving the ridiculous bag of soup.

Two mental folders: one marked 'brother' and one marked 'other'.

All the qualities that she could appreciate and enjoy about Aiden in a safe, appropriate way went in the folder marked 'brother'. Admiration for his professional aptitude, appreciation of his dry sense of humour, fascination with how he worked individuals and a whole room at the same time...

They were all perfectly wholesome things to appreciate about a sibling.

But all those less-than-wholesome feelings—the ripple of goose flesh at his touch, the tightening of her chest at his glance, the catch of her breath when he smiled, the screaming desire to get closer to him, the awful, awful *want*...

Those things went in the file marked 'other'. Not to be opened for fifty years.

It worked for about an hour.

The touching had started on the front stairs of her veranda—a gentle, scorching hand at her lower back as he directed her to his car. Then the brush of his body as he needlessly reached across her to fix her seat belt in place. Then his knuckles—curled around the gear stick of his expensive car—that somehow managed to brush the tight fabric of her skirt every time they shifted gear.

So that by the time they arrived at the restaurant, the 'other' folder was already bulging.

Then came the conversation—so witty and attentive and damned *interested* in whatever she was saying. Her Achilles heel after a father like Eric—who just wasn't interested, ever—and a boyfriend like Kyle, who struggled to fully attend to anything that didn't involve him. Those things were okay to go in the 'brother' folder, but the deep, golden glow of appreciation that started to form certainly wasn't. It was too dangerous.

She shook the 'other' folder to make some room and she shoved that in deep.

Distracting herself with exchanges with the dinner guests was a great strategy, except that she then became disturbingly conscious of his eyes on her when she was speaking with his colleagues. A cautious glance at first, then curious to see how she handled herself, then quietly pleased. And

pleasing him had her shaking that 'other' folder again to settle the contents lower.

She rolled tight shoulders. 'Must you stare at me so relent-
lessly?' she muttered sideways at him.

Something in what she said made his eyes crease and twin-
kle. 'Sorry, I'm just enjoying watching you ignoring me.'

That brought her glance back to his and she realised it
had been a long time since she'd let them make contact. 'I'm
schmoozing with your colleagues,' she said under her breath.
'Isn't that what I'm here for?'

He grew serious yet flirty at the same time. How was that
possible?

'It is. I'm not complaining.'

No. He was just locking those bedroom eyes on her and
making the 'other' folder impossible to squeeze the lid shut
on. She glanced around for a distraction but everyone else in
the room was otherwise engaged.

No rescue there.

'Why don't we sit?' Aiden indicated a vacant double-seater
in the lounge part of the restaurant.

It wasn't tiny, but a three-seater would have been more to
her liking. She sank into one side, as far over as she could
go, and cupped her drink. When Aiden sat, the entire sus-
pension of the sofa seemed to change, and she immediately
felt the slight lean of her body towards his.

As if she needed gravity's interference. She forced herself upright.

'Can I ask you about your mother?' he asked.

That brought her focus quickly back to his. 'Here?'

'You don't have to be on the job all night. I thought you
might enjoy talking about her.'

Oh. That was sweet. Her mother was so central to the difficulties between them; she was the one person they could

almost never talk about. But licence was almost crippling. 'We talk about her all the time.'

'No. We talk about *them*. What was she like? Specifically.'

It was easy to smile. Answering would have been easy, too, but Aiden wasn't asking lightly. Part of her was vaguely disturbed that he was asking at all; it seemed like strangely intimate territory for them, given what a careful line she wanted to tread. But another part of her hungered to have a normal conversation with him. Just like a regular couple—

She kicked herself mentally.

—of siblings.

'She was like me. Optimistic, perfectionist, imperfect but accepting of her own flaws and doing the best she could.'

'She must have been proud of the woman you grew into.'

Her whole body softened at the memories of the pride in her mother's eyes the first time she sold a piece. 'She was, mostly. She loved my work.'

'Mostly?'

'She wasn't thrilled with my...relationship choices.' And how she would have turned in her grave as she and someone as risky as Aiden started to get closer. 'But she recognised that I had to learn through experience. Like she did.'

It was the closest they'd come to talking about her mother and his father. As close as they'd get tonight.

'Are we talking about Jardine?'

'Mum never liked him.'

'No one likes him. Except him.'

She sat up straighter. 'He wasn't always like he is now.'

'You're defending him?'

Tash frowned. 'I think I'm defending me. Because I chose to be with him, so it reflects on me. He wasn't an ass then.'

'You just turned him into one?'

'Not intentionally.' She laughed. 'But I definitely think our relationship wasn't good for him.'

That caused his eyes to narrow a fraction. 'Why not?'

She hesitated. Just because she'd rationalised their breakup to herself didn't make her right. Her hair tickled her cheeks as she shook her head. 'I don't want you to think I'm a narcissist.'

'Why would I think that?'

She took a breath. Went for it. 'I think he was threatened by me.'

That didn't even surprise him. He nodded. 'By your success?'

'That, and...other things.'

Aiden frowned.

Oh, God, how had they arrived here? Weren't they talking about her mother just a moment ago? A warm, fuzzy, safe topic?

'We weren't all that compatible.' Tash leaned heavily enough on the last word to break it.

Again, with the blank stare. Until suddenly it wasn't blank at all. Blue eyes widened. 'Right! *Compatible.*' His lips split to reveal even white teeth. 'So Jardine is a lousy lay? That's priceless.'

'Why would you assume it's Kyle?'

'Because it's you—' the warm glow rushed in again until she batted it away with the entire crowded folder marked 'other' '—and because he told me you were a dynamo in the sack.'

The glow all but shattered, it froze so fast. 'He what?'

'Don't get angry. It was all bluster.'

'What the hell were the two of you doing having a conversation about my sexual performance in the first place?'

His hands rose in front of him as if he could physically lower the volume with which her words had erupted from her lips. He glanced around to ensure they hadn't been overheard. 'It was an introductory monologue more than a conversation and it told me more about Jardine than it did about you.'

'Except that I'm a *dynamo*.'

He slouched back against the sofa back. 'Actually "cracker" was the word he used. You should be flattered.'

'Well, I'm not.' She could totally imagine the tone with which he'd said it. It was too close to the old hurts at Kyle's hands. The implication that she was somehow aberrant.

Broken.

But she could hardly cast stones since she'd just volunteered how beige Kyle was in bed. 'I think it's time for a subject change.'

The smile didn't leave Aiden's eyes, but a curious spark formed there. Thankfully, he let it go. 'We were talking about your mother. She didn't like Kyle,' he reminded her.

'She thought he put me down to make himself feel a bigger man.'

Aiden's lips pressed tight. 'I concur with her assessment. It surprises me that you would have put up with that. You don't strike me as the type to let anyone get the better of you.'

She shrugged. 'I'm slow to learn but I get there eventually. I watched my father do the same thing to my mother and then I went out and found a man just like him.' She shook her head. 'She was delighted when I broke it off with Kyle.'

'Why did you, finally?'

'I grew up. Expected more.' Hoped for more, anyway.

His eyes took on a molten sheen. He leaned closer. 'What do you expect from a man?'

Someone who would treat her like an equal. A man who got satisfaction from watching her be the best she could be, not by trying to make her who he wanted her to be. A man who treated her as if she had value outside what she could bring him. And a man who would not blanch if she stepped out of the bathroom in something risqué.

A grown-up, in other words.

But, no. Those were not thoughts she could express aloud.

She'd shared quite enough for one evening. Especially with this man. He was just as likely to take anything she said as a job description.

And, regardless of whether or not he fitted the criteria, there was no way he was now suitable for the job.

'I expect a man who wouldn't leave his date thirsty and empty-handed,' she hedged, looking pointedly at her fingers.

Aiden smiled. 'Don't move.'

She took three long breaths in and exhaled just as slowly. She wasn't thirsty and she didn't want a drink. What she wanted was the few precious moments his departure in the direction of the restaurant's bar bought her.

'Brother' and *'other'* she repeated in her head like a man-tra.

She just had to keep her filing system going. And keep him at arm's length.

She wiped her damp palms on a restaurant napkin and curled it into a ball in her fist. Perhaps the best way to force some distance between them was to give him a return dose of the Spanish Inquisition. She had a question about him for every one he had for her. There were still lots of blanks about Aiden Moore that she'd like to see filled in. In a perfect world.

Which this wasn't.

In this flawed world, she was going to have to confront Nathaniel with her suspicions and he was going to tell Aiden that they shared genetic material. And that would be that. They'd be relegated to the polite exchange of cards at Christmas and nods across crowded parties. Because there was no way the bastard child of Nathaniel Moore would be accepted into the perfect Moore family.

Which was probably just as well, because if tonight was any indication then the only thing that was going to convince her body that Aiden was now hands-off was distance. And lots of it.

Even now, she had to concentrate to keep her heartbeat regular as he headed back across the room towards her. His suit looked even better on him from a distance. Fitted and flattering. All shoulders and lean waist. He moved like a thoroughbred.

'When is your father back?' she asked the moment Aiden returned, to keep the topic from swinging back to where they'd left it. All the relaxation fled from Aiden's body.

'His flight landed this afternoon. Back at work on Monday,' he said, sitting stiffly.

'How was their trip?'

His lips flat lined and her heart squeezed to see him swallow the pain. 'Not terribly beneficial.'

'Things are no better between them?'

'This wasn't a disagreement about finances or what colour to paint the living room, Tash. He went behind her back in seeing the daughter of a woman he'd once had an affair with and that was just too close to what he did once before.'

She softened her words to minimise the impact. 'Do you think it would have made a difference if he'd been up front with her?'

That brilliant mind turned over—and over—behind his eyes, and his response was more sigh than sentence. 'No. The hurt is in the act.' His brows dropped. 'But it's amplified by the cover-up.'

Would Laura feel any differently if she discovered it was his *daughter* he was secretly seeing? Maybe she might find it easier to forgive that? And maybe sea stars would fly.

'Better that they deal with the underlying issues, though, right?'

His eyes pierced her. 'What underlying issues?'

She regarded him steadily, welcoming the emotional gulf opening up between them. Yes, that was what they needed. Emotional distance. 'All families have underlying issues. As upsetting as this was for your mother, chances are there's other stuff going on that's really at the bottom of all of this.'

Hint hint...

'My father's poor decision-making is what's at the bottom of this.'

'Perhaps.'

His hiss was a little too loud for this refined restaurant. 'Are you a card-carrying member of the mutual admiration society, Tash?'

It was only the defensiveness in his voice that stopped hers from rising. He was particularly touchy about his mother. But it came from a very fundamental place. 'I just think you're very quick to blame him.'

'And you're very quick to defend him. And your own mother. Which only leaves one person by implication and she's the only innocent one of the lot.'

Laura Moore, innocent? The woman who stole her best friend's man at the first opportunity? Tash picked her words as carefully as if she were collecting berries from a cactus field. 'I'm not blaming your mother. I'm just suggesting that this issue might be the trigger, but it's not necessarily what the troubles between them are all about.'

'Who says there are troubles?'

She lifted one brow. 'Aiden. He had an affair.' *With his first love*. 'There must be troubles.'

'That was twenty years ago.'

'My mother died still loving him.'

'That's sad for her.'

The speed of his comeback was disturbing. And telling. But, no, she wasn't going to let him do this any longer. She needed him to pull his head out of the sand and start putting the puzzle together, and if she couldn't do it for him without breaching Nathaniel's trust then she'd have to lay out some serious breadcrumbs.

'He left her a message on her cell phone just a few months ago for what should have been her fiftieth birthday. So clearly she was still very much on his mind.'

That stopped him flat. His mind was fast enough to realise what that meant. He shook his head. 'He gave Mum his word he'd never see her again.'

'He honoured that. He didn't even go to her funeral.' Her voice cracked just slightly on that and Aiden curled his fingers around hers. She extracted them just a moment later by changing her still-full drink into the other hand. 'Since we're talking about mothers, tell me about yours. What is it about her that you love so much?'

His face grew blank. 'She's my mother.'

'You defend her so fiercely. That's very telling.'

'She's my mother,' he repeated, slower for the cognitively challenged. But then he deigned to elaborate. 'She was always there for me when my father was working. Taking me to school, making my lunches, salving my wounds, mixing with my friends' mothers, which helped me to fit in, volunteering in class.'

Something inside her squeezed. 'You didn't fit in at school? Did you struggle making friends?'

'On the contrary.' She thought that was going to be it, but then he surprised her with a rare moment of candour. 'But I struggled keeping them.'

She didn't find that hard to picture. He would have been charismatic even as a boy, but his high expectations when it came to others must have meant constant disappointment in the friend department.

'I was seven when the whole Moore v. Porter thing began, so I grew up knowing something bad happened, and it happened because of my father.' His eyes beseeched her. 'But it happened *to* my mother, you know?'

Laura—always the victim...despite getting her man, and a

beautiful son, and the luxurious lifestyle and everything that brought with it. But Tash forced herself to be charitable. 'It's right that you love her so much—'

'Thanks for the permission.'

'—but you're also an adult, so you should be able to look at both of them with adult eyes.'

The eyes in question narrowed. 'What is it that you think I'm not seeing?'

Uh-oh. One breadcrumb too many. 'Just…there's always more to the story.'

He stared so long and so hard she wondered if things were about to turn dangerous. But then his brows folded—just a hint—and the cogs started turning behind his eyes. 'I'll keep that in mind. Right now, I wouldn't mind hearing more of the story we were just discussing. Your story.'

Instantly her body tightened up as her mind shut down.

'My story is not all that exciting.'

'Only child, estranged from asshole dad, dumps jerk boyfriend and loses beloved mother in the space of a couple of years. So who does Natasha Sinclair turn to when things get bad?'

Tash pressed back into the sofa back. 'She turns inward. Finds the strength in herself.'

'That's very Zen of you.'

'It's also true.' She chuckled. 'Though I will admit to asking myself what Mum would do in situations I can't handle.'

He shifted only slightly but it seemed to bring him—and his mesmerising lips—much closer. 'I can't imagine there's anything you can't handle.'

Dangerously close. But she worked around the danger as best she could. 'You might be surprised. Situations where I only have two choices and both of them are bad.'

'Bad for whom?'

'For the people involved. Bad for me.'

'And what do you do then?'

'I just navigate my way through it.'

'You don't ever want to just offload on someone? Share the burdens of life?'

Oh, my God…did she ever. She used to do that with her mum. 'That would be a bad reason to commence a relationship. Just to have someone to decompress with.'

His lips twisted. 'There are worse reasons.'

'What do you know about sharing?' she asked, her curiosity well and truly piqued by the strangeness of his expression. 'You're the most island-like of men that I know.'

'We were talking about you.'

'We might as well have been talking about you; we're quite similar,' she mused.

Without warning, he reached out and caressed a single lock of her hair with his index finger. Tash forced herself not to flinch. 'We are. I've noticed that. Not in the detail, but in the essential things.'

There's a reason we're so similar, she wanted to scream. Instead, she leaned forward and placed her glass on the small table in front of their sofa, subtly dislodging his touch. Or at least effectively. 'I have my aunt Karen. And friends.'

'You have friends?'

Her laugh was immediate. 'Of course I do. Did you imagine I just inflate a few minutes before you walk in the room? I have a lot of art friends, and a couple of school friends I'm still close to.'

'Why don't you ever talk about them?'

'Because we don't talk about ordinary things like friends. We only talk about safe things.' Or dangerous things.

'We talked tonight.'

Yes, and the timing was exquisite irony. 'Even that had an agenda.'

'What agenda?'

'You're buttering me up. Making up for bringing me out this evening.'

'From your deathbed?'

'Okay, I possibly wasn't as sick as I made out, but this has hardly been casual conversation. Are you trying to lull me into a false sense of security?'

His eyes grew serious. 'I'm trying to get to know you, Tash.'

'In Braille?' He had to know all that touching was getting heavy-handed.

A tiny splotch of red appeared halfway up his tanned throat. 'Was it that bad?'

'It's not *bad*.' Though it couldn't be good, now. 'It's just obvious.'

'I confess I'm not usually in this position.' The words were grudging and Tash got the sense that they'd never crossed his lips before. 'Having to work at keeping the conversation going. The women I date usually take care of the chat. Or they just don't bother.'

Her chest squeezed. 'Is this a date?'

'I don't know what this is. It's a mystery.'

It grew impossible to remember the difference between the two folders. 'A pleasing mystery or a count-the-minutes-until-it's-over mystery?' she breathed, hypnotised by the way his eyes turned smoky.

'Do you see me looking at my watch?'

'Consider me an education, then. Maybe this is how the real people do it.'

'As opposed to the fake people?'

'You're not fake, you just don't move on the same plane as everyone else. Or by the same rules.'

'And you don't like that?'

She couldn't afford to. 'I do like that, actually. But I don't trust it.'

'You mean you don't trust *me*.'

'I don't trust anyone.'

'Why not?'

'Experience. But I trust you more than most, so that's something.'

'You trusted me the other day, lying on the edge of the water.'

It was impossible not to be honest with him. Despite the 'other' folder. That day was one of the nicest she'd had in ages. 'I saw the real you that day.'

'Did you like what you saw?'

It was there, sheltering right at the back of his eyes behind all the arrogance.

Uncertainty.

But she wasn't about to kick a man on his way to being down. Besides, hope had a place in both folders. And she was the first to acknowledge that even the perpetually positive had their demons. 'You are an amazing man, Aiden Moore. Handsome and rich and available.' *Until the next sure thing came along.* 'I'd be a fool not to recognise it.'

His eyes narrowed.

'But I like you best when you're not trying so hard. When I don't feel like part of the latest angle you're playing. Or, worse, part of some kind of set-up I don't yet understand.'

His long, silent stare graduated into a slow, appreciative nod. 'I'm amazed Jardine came away able to function at all. I would have expected that kind of insight to neuter a man like him.'

Her breath twisted into a painful ball in her chest. But he saw the flare of her nostrils and hurried to continue. 'Don't get me wrong. That's very definitely his failing, not yours. You've said nothing that isn't true—to my shame—and you said it very carefully. But it's not an easy thing being so transparent when you're more accustomed to obsequiousness.'

Tash curled her fingers into her lap. 'If I had such great insight then I should know what this play is.' But she didn't. What was he doing now? 'I can't read you.'

'Maybe because I'm being genuine. I *was* playing you this evening. I wanted to stroke you into submission, ease the nerves I assumed you were feeling.'

'Feeling about what?'

'About us. Tonight. About where we were going. But that was just wishful thinking on my part. We weren't going there at all, were we?'

She stared at him and gave two answers. One for each folder.

'No. But that's not to say I haven't enjoyed your company or our conversation.' That was for the potential brother she didn't want to wound. 'And it's not to say I mightn't have chosen differently earlier in the week.' And that was because she had to be true to herself. Although she protected herself by being safely cryptic.

'You want the bad news?' Aiden said after a long, awkward silence. Tash shrugged. 'This candour isn't making me want you any less.'

He couldn't want her. It was that simple. If—no, when!—he found out why, he'd look back at all these moments with humiliated fury. But he didn't have to remember her making it worse. Or making a scene.

She flattened her skirt and stood decisively. 'Apparently unattainability is part of my charm.'

He joined her on his feet. 'You think you're charming? That's sweet.'

It was still flirting, but everything had shifted gear these past few minutes. Into safer territory. As if the shark were increasing the diameter of its circles. Giving her room to breathe. Respectful, kind room.

'You know what else is sweet?' he murmured, guiding her to rejoin the other guests.

She cast him a curious look.

'You think this is over, too.'

This *was* over. It had to be. Otherwise the hurt was going to be too profound.

Tash glanced at her watch. Ten o'clock. She spun on him. 'You said your father got back today?'

'Back at work Monday.'

'We need to see him.'

That stopped him in his tracks. 'What?'

'We need to speak with your father. Now.'

'Why?'

'When we speak to him, you'll understand. This has gone on long enough.' She gathered her handbag closer to her—like armour—shaking but determined. 'Can you call him?'

'Are you okay, Tash? You've lost all your colour. Please don't tell me you were sick all along....'

'I'm fine.'

'Maybe I should take you home—'

'Call your father, Aiden. Get him to meet us at MooreCo.' The offices would be abandoned this time on a Friday night. They'd have total privacy.

He reached for his phone. 'Tash. What's going on?'

'I'll explain when we get there.' She took his arm a smidge more forcefully than she meant and steered him towards the door. 'Come on.'

Time to end this.

CHAPTER TEN

'I'M WHAT?'

Aiden's incredulous rasp cut across the top of Nathaniel's astonished gasp. 'Tash—'

'Half-brother, really,' she rushed, holding Aiden's blue eyes. It was hard to tell which man was the palest.

'Natasha—' Nathaniel croaked.

She turned to him. 'I'm sorry if this makes things more difficult for you, Nathaniel. But he had to know.'

Nathaniel's eyes dropped and he murmured, 'Oh, God...'

'Do you have any idea what it was like for me, growing up with him?' she begged, unable to hold it in any longer. 'Believing my own father hated me?' Yet that thought was painfully validating. She'd never believed that a true father could possibly loathe his own offspring. It had to be biologically impossible. 'And all along...'

She didn't need to finish. She needed to stop talking, let the men process.

Aiden's horrified stare moved between the two of them, but his accusations finally landed on his father. 'Your affair started before I was even born?'

Tash's breath puffed out of her in an angry hiss. 'Seriously? That's what you're taking from this?'

I'm your sister!

'It wasn't an affair then,' Nathaniel defended, his focus entirely on Aiden.

'Semantics,' Aiden barked.

Nathaniel's mouth flattened in a way that was so like his son's. 'No. Not when you're casting judgement as you are. Your mother and I had parted when I got back together with Adele.'

'After you got Mum pregnant?'

'Yes, as it turns out.'

'And then you got Porter pregnant, too?' Aiden cut in.

Nathaniel paused, and then turned to Tash, his eyes full of grief. 'No.'

'Yes!'

He curled a creased hand around her wrist and just held it. As if his skin over her pulse would help lessen the impact of what he was saying. 'No, Tash. I am not your father.'

Grief such as she hadn't felt since losing her mother welled up and voiced in her croak. 'Yes…you are.'

He didn't deny it again, he just slid his fingers lower, to thread through hers.

'You were together,' she wobbled. 'You slept with Laura to get back at Mum. You were angry at her.'

Aiden's gasp was audible. 'Is that true?' He came around to Tash's other side so he could see his father's face.

Nathaniel's eyes fell shut. 'It's true. Adele and I had fought and I went with Laura to get back at her. To make a point.'

Aiden's entire body froze up.

'But then you were with her again,' Tash urged. 'After Laura.'

'Yes, but we never…' Nathaniel took a long deep breath. 'We were never together, Tash. Physically.'

Aiden snorted.

Nathaniel rounded on him. 'Well might you scoff, Aiden. With the choices you make and the women you seek out, it wouldn't occur to you that two people could be desperately in love and never consummate it.'

'Bull.'

'Not everyone lives their life quite as fast as you do, son.' Then he turned away again, dismissing his own flesh, and focused on Tash. 'Your mother was wild and crazy in some ways, but she was traditional in one way that really counted.'

'You never slept together?' Tash croaked.

'It's why we broke up in the first place.'

Tash lifted her lashes. Her eyes burned with unshed tears. 'Because she wouldn't sleep with you?'

Shame etched into his handsome features. 'I was young. Stupid. And I made a beeline for the first person I knew would. To hurt Adele as much as I was hurting.'

'You son of a bitch.' The insult spewed from Aiden and Nathaniel spun on him again.

'You know what, son? I've lived with your judgement for twenty years. From the moment you got old enough to form an opinion, you've held one of me—a bad one—without knowing any of the facts. I've let that ride *because* you didn't have the facts and because I could see how much validation you got from being your mother's champion and how much of *her* world revolved around your good opinion. But I've more than done my time. I walked away from the woman I loved to do the right thing by your mother when I got her pregnant. I stood by her even knowing that she—'

The sudden silence drew Tash's eyes up again.

'Even knowing what?'

Nathaniel's lips pressed impossibly harder. 'Even knowing that I'd never see Adele again.'

'Why did you?'

'Because whatever I chose I was going to ruin someone's life. It might as well have been my own.'

Aiden blanched as pale as the ivory trim of his expensive tie. He flopped into the nearest chair. 'Right.'

'No,' Nathaniel sighed, seeing immediately which way Aiden's mind was going. 'I never blamed you and I never felt that way about you. I had a *son*, the only consolation in an otherwise miserable period. But choosing your mother over Adele had nothing to do with my feelings for her and everything to do with penance for what a bastard I'd been, pressuring Adele for more than she was ready for.'

'Does Laura know?' Tash whispered, her first pang of sympathy for her mother's rival.

'She knew in her heart at the time. And she knew for sure after…' His eyes found the horizon out of the window. 'But I'd never fully committed to her until the truth was exposed.'

'Why didn't you go with Mum when she was finally free?'

His hands rose to his side and then fell, defeated. 'Because I'd committed to Laura. And I realised I'd kept her in stasis for eight years. I couldn't then abandon her.'

'A bit late for chivalry, wasn't it?' Aiden snorted, and his father locked eyes with him.

'I chose your mother, Aiden. Freely. Twice. But I will not lie to you that I loved her the way I loved Tash's mother. Adele Porter was—and will always be—my heart.'

Nathaniel's voice cracked and Tash's tears spilled over. It took them both a moment to get their emotion under control.

'Think it through, Tash,' Nathaniel said gently, stroking her hair. 'Adele would have told you, if she thought you were mine. Before she died. Wouldn't she?'

The sense of that filtered through her confusion. Yeah. She would have. She had a long, lingering death to share the most important information in the world. A detail like that would certainly have qualified.

But she wasn't ready to nod. Not just yet. She was still grieving.

'I would be the proudest man on earth to say I was the father to two such amazing children and I would have given anything to know that my child was growing in Adele's body. And to have saved you the misery of your childhood with Eric.' He bent to engage her lowered eyes. 'But I give you my absolute word, we never had sex and so you cannot be mine.'

There really was no doubt in his tone. No room for misunderstanding. But still she hoped in a tiny voice, 'But we're so similar.'

'We are. I've noticed it too. I wonder whether it's your mother's traits you have and maybe she picked some of them up from me all those years ago.'

'I have your eyes.' Desperation was such a terrible optimist.

His laugh was gentle. 'You have *brown* eyes, Tash. Along with half the planet. Including your aunt Karen, if I remember rightly.'

She made a desperate, final-ditch plea. 'You warned me off Aiden…'

'Because he's so damaged—'

'Hey!' Aiden's head snapped up from where he was lost in the plush carpet at their feet.

'I would give my life for yours, son, but you're the product of my dysfunctional relationship with your mother. You learned your values about love and trust from a very imperfect example. I see the legacy of that every single day.'

Aiden's nostrils flared, but respect kept him silent.

'I so wanted to be your daughter,' Tash whispered.

He turned back to her. Pulled her to him, right up into his shoulder, and murmured, 'I know.'

'But I was torn,' she whispered against his ear. 'Because of Aiden.'

His arms tightened. 'Please be careful, Tash.'

She let his words sink in. She thought back to her own

family, how much damage her parents' dysfunctional relationship had done. But how much more might have been done if they had stayed together. And Aiden had grown up in that environment. Long, impressionable years. Empathy washed through her.

She pulled back. 'Thank you for validating her,' she murmured.

'I wish it could have been more.'

Aiden pushed to his feet. 'I need to…some air. I'm going home.'

'You're my ride,' she stammered, needing escape but needing to not be alone just yet. And more than a little bit worried for Aiden. This was all a massive shock to him, once again.

'I'll work with Max to cover your appointments,' Nathaniel volunteered, concerned brown eyes on his son. 'Take a few days off.'

Aiden spun back and if he was going to say something sharper, he changed his mind. 'Thank you,' he simply murmured instead.

'You're welcome.'

God, so painfully polite. She thought back to all those altercations with her cold, cutting father the few times she'd had to see him as an adult. Moments rather like this one.

'Are you okay?' she asked Aiden as they waited for the elevator, wanting to touch him but not daring.

He didn't even look at her. 'My head feels like it's going to explode.'

'It's a lot to take in.'

'I'm not sure who I feel more betrayed by—him or you.'

She turned to him. 'How could I tell you? It had to be him.'

'You've known all week. This is why you were so weird about the party.'

'I suspected.'

'You thought I was your *brother*. What the hell were you doing coming out with me at all?'

'You came to my house.'

'You should have just told me to hit the road.'

'I'm not very skilled in that kind of brush-off, strange as it might seem to you. I handled it as best I could under the circumstances.'

Surely, he couldn't fail to remember the many different ways she'd kept him at arm's length.

'Must have been highly entertaining for you to watch me hitting on my own sister.'

That would have stung if she'd thought for a moment he meant it. 'It was awful. I wanted to tell you, I wanted to share the information and the anxiety and have someone I could talk to about it. I thought I had a whole other family.' Her voice tightened. 'I was so excited.'

And yet dreading it at the same time because of what it meant for them.

His eyes slid down to hers. Softened. 'But you don't.'

Her heart sank. 'No. I'm back to being alone.'

Aiden considered his words. 'I saw the way my father just was with you. Whatever happens I don't think you'll be alone. If he could have fathered you I know he would have.'

Tash concentrated on the changing elevator numbers above them, blinking back moisture. Had they always moved this slowly?

'You're lucky, you know,' she eventually said. 'To have him.'

'Really? A workaholic adulterer incapable of loving the mother of his child?'

Pain seeped from his words. 'I'm not saying it's not a tragedy. But he's a good man, no matter what he's done in the past. He saved my mother's life. And mine, probably. And he did the right thing by Laura. Twice.'

'It's good to see that you have such a strong streak for forgiveness. You might even be able to see past *my* apparently numerous imperfections.'

'He loves you, Aiden. He's just worried for you.'

His dark head shook.

'We wouldn't be human if we didn't have flaws, Aiden.'

'Really?' He rounded on her. 'What are yours?'

Tash shrugged. 'I say what I think way too readily. I believe in the best in others even after I've experienced their worst.'

'Is that a polite way of saying you're gullible?'

'I mean for a girl who had my upbringing I'm surprisingly fast to trust.'

His snort echoed around the large, empty parking floor as they stepped out into it. 'You must be joking.'

'What?'

'It took me weeks to earn your trust. I consider it somewhat of a milestone the day I did.'

'What day was that?'

'The paddle boats. So it was a short honeymoon.'

'Perhaps some people just shouldn't be trusted.'

His tight lips split into a wolfish smile. 'Oh, honey... Truer words have never been spoken.'

They fell to silence for the bulk of the journey back to her cottage, his eyes grazing her periodically.

'You realise what today means?' he finally said, pulling into her street.

She dragged her eyes back from faraway thoughts. 'That I'm not the bastard child of a good man.' She was just the good child of a bastard.

His eyes shimmered for a half-breath, compassionate and understanding, but then he pulled up outside her gate, turned sideways on his luxury leather seat and faced her fully. 'Today means we're not related. Today means there's no reason we can't be together. Unless you have another hurdle queued up for me.'

'I didn't set this one up, intentionally.'

'It was convenient though, wasn't it? To keep me at a safe distance. What will keep you safe now?'

She stared at him. 'That's the thing, Aiden. I do feel safe with you.'

'You did say you were too quick to trust.'

The laugh burst out of her, reluctant and grudging. 'Your idea of flirting is kind of screwy.'

He slid an arm across behind her seat. 'This isn't flirting, honey. It's foreplay.'

And that was working, too. The whole bad-boy-with-prom-ise-in-his-eye thing had her pulse racing and her palms damp-ening. And it was impossible to forget that she'd got one secret wish even while being denied the other.

Aiden was not her brother. No shared DNA.

She practically tumbled out of the car and up her short garden path. Aiden followed her up the couple of steps to her house. At the door, she unlocked it and then turned to face him. 'Thank you for the ride.'

He lifted one brow. 'I'm coming in.'

Her breath tightened up in her chest. 'I thought you wanted some thinking space.'

'Change of plans. I have no interest in thinking about any of it. Not right now.'

'You can't just avoid it.'

'Yeah, I can.' He pressed her back against the door and whispered against her lips just before his touched hers. 'Watch me.'

His lips descending towards hers were like a homecom-ing. She'd wanted this—and loathed herself because of it. Her body clearly knew the truth even as her mind couldn't accept it. But now there *was* nothing standing in the way of the kiss she wasn't even trying to run from.

Her lungs inflated just as he sealed her mouth with his, the soft, firm, heavenly pressure causing a riot in her nerve endings. The warmth of his skin against hers, the tickle of his breath and the pressure of his arms as they circled behind her. The firm press of hard body against soft.

And the insane explosion of the chemistry that zinged between them. It surged through her system, triumphant at finally being able to express itself, and pooled in her lower half, robbing her legs of strength. She twisted her arms up around the neck she had no good reason not to twist around, and kissed the lips that she had no good reason not to kiss.

And she was lost—the moment she tasted him.

The moment she felt his tongue and lips lapping against her own, exploring and teasing. Her body rejoiced at being back in his arms again; this man she'd believed she'd never be able to look in the eye, let alone kiss.

Her head actually spun with all the blood rushing to it and away again.

'Inside,' he mumbled against her lips.

His arm at her waist released her long enough to fumble around behind her lower back, before tightening again and supporting her as the door swung inwards.

She stumbled back into her own living room, shunted by the steam engine that was Aiden, and he kicked the door shut behind them. Every part of her wanted to launch at him, to press him back against the wall and climb all over him. But old fear held her back, and she waited to see what his next move would be. But not for long. As soon as the door clicked into place he forked his long fingers into her hair, pulling it back from the feverish face he framed between his palms. He stared into her eyes, one thumb sliding over to make sure her lips didn't get lonely as he spoke. 'I've wanted this since we met.'

'So, not just physical, then?' she breathed, amazed that a coherent thought could form, let alone a facetious one. Then she bit into the soft pad of his thumb—unable to ignore it any longer—and he pressed the advantage, sliding it into her mouth and out again as his lips returned.

'Minx.' He kissed her, long, hard and drugged. 'If it was just physical it would have been much easier to ignore.'

The implication provoked her but she wasn't about to indulge it. 'You don't strike me as a man accustomed to self-deprivation.'

Yep. Because this was the right time for conversation. But if she didn't ease back on the throttle this was going to go a little bit too fast and a little bit too furious. And—though she'd longed for something faster and more furious than Kyle and though the promise of Aiden's strength spiced her blood— she wanted to savour every moment. In case they were the only moments she ever got.

He tugged on her hair enough to expose the long line of her throat and he murmured into her skin, 'Just one of my many depravations.'

She laughed gently at the wordplay. 'Oh, really? What are some others?'

He smiled against her flesh and moved his lips to her ear, hot and seductive. 'We have all night for those.'

And then his hands left her hair and made their way down her body, stroking and exciting her nerve endings as they went. Every man she'd ever been with had had a heavy touch—demanding, rushed, or clumsy. But Aiden traced the lines of her body as if it were one of her own artworks, discovering her, savouring. Then he took her hands and pinned them behind her body, which he pressed against hard, holding her captive.

The contrast between his feather-light touch and his sheer command boiled her blood even more. She'd had a taste of his strength in the coatroom, and she'd liked it. And she'd wanted to match it. But it wouldn't be the first time she'd misread someone's intent. It was too easy to remember Kyle's shock when she'd stepped up to the sensual challenge *he'd* posed and then quailed when she'd taken the cue.

Literally quailed. He'd scrabbled backwards from her in his expensive, overly stuffed bed, flushed and uncomfortable, and been sure to dominate any encounter the two of them ever had after that. Not in a good way. In an afraid-of-your-own shadow kind of way. And that was *not* sexy. It had made her feel dirty and ashamed for rising so enthusiastically to meet Kyle's sexual bravado that had turned out to be all show.

As if she needed any help with shame.

But Aiden wasn't Kyle. Far from it. The signals he was sending seemed crystal in their clearness and unshakeable in intent. And he'd spoken before of liking a woman who was bold.

Lord knew she hungered to be bold.

Dare she take this chance? Was that the kind of bold he was really looking for? Someone who took the initiative?

She forced strength into the arms pinned behind her back and circled them up above her head and then back down in front of her. Aiden immediately eased his weight back, letting her escape, but as she brought them back down she shoved him clean in the middle of his chest.

Hard.

He regained his footing against the door, panting, watching her intently. She stood, chest heaving, desperately trying to read his closed expression, and then she did exactly what she'd wanted to since he first stood in the doorway to her workshop, judging her. She pursued him to the wall, pushed him back against it with a thud and tore his shirt open, buttons pinging everywhere.

Outing herself in as graphic a fashion as she could possibly have *not* wanted to do.

It was the inwards suck of breath that drew her eyes up to his. She hoped it would be surprise and not shock, not dismay. Definitely not anxiety. But she didn't expect to see the roasting glow of unfettered desire as he challenged, 'You owe me a shirt.'

No judgement. No distaste. Just...*want*.

The push of his strong shoulder muscles against the wall was enough to propel them both into the centre of the room, towards the sofa that divided the open space into two parts. As the back of Tash's thighs hit the upholstered rear of the sofa, she braced herself on its top and met the furious kiss that Aiden meted out.

Met it and matched it.

She curled her fingers into the destroyed remains of his shirt and pulled him towards her, bending backwards over the furniture. One masculine hand stabilised next to her hip and the other fisted in her hair, and he resisted long enough to stare hotly into her eyes.

'You want to drive?' he questioned softly.

Her heart hammered so hard it was almost pain, but she embraced even that.

This was it. The defining moment she'd always hoped for. A good man—a beautiful man—giving her control and giving her licence. Creating a safe environment in which to test her limits and offering himself up as her crash test dummy. She had thought that moment just a minute ago was the big risk: turning the tables and revealing this aspect of herself to Aiden, but articulating it—*taking* the control he was offering—was so much more terrifying.

Because she wanted it so much. And because it meant she wasn't broken after all.

She just hadn't yet found her equal.

Astute Aiden read her hesitation. 'I'll look after you,' he vowed, his molten gaze committed.

And he would. She knew it instinctively. Because that was the man he was. All those qualities that split the seams of the bulging 'brother' folder hadn't diminished now that he was officially an 'other'. His intelligence, his compassion and focus and interest in anything new and challenging, his spirit and his loyalty and values. All the things that had wheedled in under her skin and made him so hard to walk away from. They were highlighted—amplified—by the desire now pumping off him in waves, but they weren't overruled.

Aiden Moore would look after her until the day he died if he let himself. Look at his concern for his mother. He was a keeper.

It was why she'd fallen for him.

She stared up into the simmering pools of igneous blue as everything fell into place with an inevitable *thunk*. That was why she felt so connected to him. That was why the threat of having to walk away had hurt so much. That was why she felt safe enough in his arms to expose her deepest secret.

She loved him.

He stroked a loose lock of hair back from her face as if sensing her turmoil, not pushing, but not retreating. Just… waiting.

She took a deep breath. And poured all her trust into her smile.

And reached for him.

CHAPTER ELEVEN

HAD THERE EVER been anything quite as beautiful as this moment? Tash spread gloriously naked across her bed. Unconscious. Inelegant. Vulnerable.

All things she would hate most.

And mine.

The word just kept floating back across Aiden's consciousness no matter how hard he worked to push it away. He loved to make someone his. To brand them. To win them even against their better judgement because they just couldn't help themselves. A besting.

But, no, this wasn't that kind of 'mine'.

This was a whole other beast. A rabid, jealous, protective kind of 'mine'. The kind of mine that made him want to tiptoe out of here, hunt down Eric Sinclair and slice his belly three ways before morning for hurting her so badly. Or get him arrested and let the other incarcerated filth have at him.

Or even deck his own father for *not* being hers as well. Simply because she'd wanted it so very much and some part of him had suddenly decided that protecting Tash and meeting her needs was now his job. Which was ridiculous. *She'd* deck *him* for even thinking it.

That was not what they were about.

He backed away from the doorway and returned to the kitchen to see if the coffee was ready yet. He'd sought refuge in the kitchen because he didn't trust himself to lie half sprawled under her and not reach for her again. And she'd earned a rest, God knew.

His beautiful, wild Tash.

No, not *his*. He'd never had a stronger urge to make that clear to the stars peppering the sky. What they'd just done, what they'd just been to each other was a partnership. Two equals. And that was new for him.

And more than a little bit unsettling.

His father had called him 'damaged'—charming!—but while his past relationships were about expediency, they were also with decent women. Women who wanted a similar, brief, no-strings exchange. Not quite as special or unique as Tash, granted, but it wasn't as if he'd picked them up on some street corner.

Sex and power were so intertwined. And he liked to control the power, ergo he controlled the sex. When it happened, where it happened, who it happened with. He might have ceded some of that control to Tash tonight but he'd taken it back by the end of the night, until she begged for his touch. He always did. The physical aspects, the emotional aspects. All tightly marshalled. That was how he liked it. And time was the greatest co-driver a man could have. The shorter the relationship, the more control he wielded.

Amen.

And you know what...? Daddy dearest really wasn't in a position to criticise his relationship choices given how he'd treated the two most significant women in his life.

Pot. Kettle. Black.

Speaking of which...Aiden flipped the switch on the now fully percolated coffee and splashed a healthy amount plain into one of Tash's mugs. He'd accepted he wasn't going to sleep again tonight—his mind was way too busy even as his body wanted him to tumble into satiated slumber—so coffee it was. Black. Strong. And lots of it.

It did only a partial job of purging the guilt he still felt for being so weak.

Ironic that someone who embraced the challenge of corporate conflict so heartily should struggle as he did with personal conflict. But deep-and-meaningful discussions weren't really done in his family. In his case, he'd also refined the art of finding something—or someone—to convincingly steal focus. And since he'd hit puberty that something was sexual.

Like tonight.

He should have been at home, unable to sleep, working his way through the emotional minefield that was his messed-up family, not here, making Tash into a human displacement activity.

Using her.

The guilt nibbled again. This wasn't a small deal for her. He'd seen how she struggled to open up with him and let her raw sensuality out. And he knew she didn't sleep around casually. And—just in case he was missing the point—the universe rammed it home just half an hour ago when her beautiful, exhausted eyes had fluttered open and locked on his for seconds and then fluttered shut again. In that unguarded moment, she'd completely failed to disguise a blazing kind of intensity saturating the chocolate pools.

A kind of half-asleep worship.

He'd practically scrabbled out from under her, the big thumping muscle in his chest near exploding. Because it had almost looked like—

No, he wouldn't go there. Going there had consequences.

He sipped the scalding coffee as his eyes trailed over the explosion of bright, happy photographs stuck to Tash's fridge, trying to piece together a timeline of her happiest moments. Moments of joy. Moments of love. He got another flash of those chocolate eyes blazing into his with such…sleepy optimism. He drank a gulp so hot his eyes literally watered, and it banished all other thought effectively away.

He'd faced this moment of realisation many times in the past. It was part of his process. It was also why he never brought anyone back to his place. If you're in your own place you can't leave. And he left the moment things turned sticky. The moment he got the slightest sense that the woman he was with was getting entangled.

Or, in this case, *he* was.

The very fact it was happening against his better judgement meant it shouldn't happen at all. He stared at the biggest of the photographs on the refrigerator. Tash with her mother, somewhere beachy, both blissfully happy.

The Porter-Sinclair women.

The most unsuitable woman in the world for him if he also wanted to have any kind of relationship with his mother. Which he did. She'd been abandoned enough by men for one lifetime. He wasn't about to add to that.

His eyes drifted upwards to the top of the fridge and then froze as they encountered a translucent bluey-orange leg, complete with a series of delicate nubs beneath it, bent over the top edge of the white appliance. A chubby little sea star, with its perfect sucker feet and almost living appearance. He touched one of his fingers to one of its.

His starfish. The exact same one he'd watched her make yesterday. How was it even possible that so much could have changed in thirty-six hours? He'd been sure that this little guy would end up in the shards bucket on principle; she'd thrust it into that cooling kiln with such perfunctory disinterest. As if it was valueless to her.

Yet, here it was. Squirreled away in her house.

It dawned on him then that, for a woman who made her living working with glass, this little starfish was woefully outnumbered in her cottage. Which made its presence painfully significant. He took its slight weight in the palm of his hand and let those cool, hard legs hang off the edge of his hand into space. It was far from perfect—the legs were irregular and its colours not evenly distributed. Then again, Tash had made it under duress. But, overall, he found the flaws, partly hidden by the smooth beauty of the glass, rather appealing.

It reminded him of him.

Except he liked to think he did a much better job of disguising his flaws.

But then the reality sank in: women didn't collect things like that for no reason, at least not practical women like Tash. If she'd been planning on giving it to him, she would have done so earlier when he picked her up for dinner. So that meant she was keeping it as a memento—his chest tightened up hard—and that wasn't good news.

The keepsake put that honey-blast she'd fired at him from her beautiful chocolate pools into a whole new light. And the trust she'd shown in revealing her wild side, too. And just about every smile and glance she'd sent his way these past weeks. It meant they weren't the casual kind of looks, or smiles, or actions that you just walked away from. Responsibility surged in thick and awful as he stared down at the little fella in his hands. Then up at the fridge.

Yeah, the starfish was him, all right. And Tash had put it where she displayed her most precious memories.

Which meant it was time to leave.

And the sheer force of his desire not to meant that he absolutely had to.

Funny how a bed could feel empty even when it normally was. After just a few hours of cohabitation.

Tash stirred into wakefulness, skirting her fingers over the cool sheets beside her and forcing gritty eyes open. Five in the morning was not enough sleep at the best of times, never mind when several hours had been occupied with intense, exhausting physical activity. She trained her ears to her left, towards the en suite.

Nothing.

Frowning, she pushed her pleasantly aching muscles into a half-upright position.

'Aiden?' she murmured, holding back with forced positivity the chill that wanted so badly to settle.

He hadn't left. He hadn't.

He wouldn't do that to her.

She switched on the bedside lamp and glanced around, breath suspended, for a hastily scrawled note. Nothing. She flipped over on a groan and swung her feet to the floor, before sliding on her robe to further keep the chill at bay. Was no note good news or bad news? Did it mean he hadn't left or he *had* but didn't feel obliged to even tell her? Absence in a house this small was a rather self-evident thing, if you looked. And Aiden was a logical guy.

Just look! She scolded herself, wishing she was cool and collected enough not to need to; the sort of person who could have just rolled over in bed and gone back to sleep. Eight o'clock would have been a much better time to be having this crisis of confidence.

Light footfalls took her out into the living area.

Nothing. But her nose told her everything she needed to know.

'Needed the caffeine?' she murmured, stepping into the entry to the kitchen.

Aiden stood in front of her refrigerator, staring at the clutter pinned to it with cheerful magnets. Behind him through the window, the navy sky sat heavy as her heart. As he turned, Tash glanced at the coffee pot and saw the remnants of the high tide mark ringing the glass.

That had to be at least three refills given the size of the mug he'd borrowed. How long had he been out here staring at her fridge?

When her eyes returned to Aiden's, his were guarded. And intensely apologetic.

The chill officially won.

'Oh.'

It was all she could manage past the sudden gridlock in her throat. It seemed incredibly inevitable now and she wondered how she could possibly not have seen this coming last night. But here it was.

The moment.

'How are you feeling?' he murmured.

She didn't want him asking that. *How are you feeling?* implied he gave a toss. *How are you feeling?* suggested she'd done something she should have felt awkward about. *How are you feeling?* was a prelude to *Well, I should be going.*

'What happened, couldn't work the inside deadlock?' she asked, folding her arms across her chest.

His lips pressed together. 'I wasn't leaving.'

'Overdosing on caffeine instead seems a bit extreme.'

His smile didn't deserve to warm her. 'I wanted to wait until you woke up.'

But you are leaving? 'I'm awake now.'

'Why are you?'

Because you weren't there and the absence felt wrong. She might as well tattoo 'high maintenance' to her forehead. 'It's odd to have someone else in the house. I must have sensed you moving around.'

He didn't believe her and she didn't blame her.

'So...this is a world record,' she squeezed out, hideously brightly, 'even for me. Is there such a thing as a half-night stand?'

His eyes fell shut. 'Tash—'

'No, I get it. Now. I didn't really get it before, though. The way you looked at me earlier…'

Ugh. She *so* didn't want to be one of those women that said 'but I thought'. But she really *had* thought.

'I shouldn't have come here.' He shook his mussed-up head. 'We shouldn't have slept together.'

She blinked at him and tightened her arms one more notch. So maybe she was broken after all. She'd come on way too strong and freaked him out. Though she'd truly believed him un-freakable. He was Aiden Moore. A man with his reputation had to have encountered stranger than her.

'Nobody forced you,' she defended, and then got an instant visual of her slamming him against the wall and buttons flying around them both. 'Initially.'

'I care for you, Tash. And I knew this wasn't going further so I shouldn't have started it. It wasn't fair of me.'

She stared at him and heard echoes of Kyle and even her father. Making lame excuses. Taking responsibility in the patronising, masculine way that made it patently clear it was secretly all her fault. As if they were doing her some kind of favour. It was beneath a man like Aiden and she was offended *for* him as much as *by* him.

She nodded and turned to leave the kitchen, as dignified as she could manage, but at the last minute the social justice campaigner in her—the part that wasn't much troubled by dignity or lack of it—forced her to speak.

She spun back from the doorway. 'Sorry… *Why* isn't this going further exactly?'

'Tash, don't do this.'

Every part of her tightened.

'Hold you accountable for your actions?' Suddenly she very much wanted to hear what he had to say, precisely because it was unpleasant for him to say it. She shouldn't be the only one feeling the pressure here. 'All those lusty stares, the coatroom kiss, the paddle-boat day...I would have thought you have had plenty of opportunity to have a crisis of conscience.'

Come on, Aiden, say it. Even Kyle-the-gutless had managed to say it. *You came on too strong, Tash.* Just as she had with Kyle. Just as she had with her father the one time she tried—really tried, but failed—to find some common ground with him and begin patching their fatally flawed relationship.

Seemed like try-hard was just her thing.

'You looked like you were enjoying yourself,' she gritted. And he'd willingly given her control. Did he not expect her to actually take it?

'This isn't about tonight, Tash.'

Of course it was. She'd been here before. Stupid her for imagining this time would be different. 'Then what's it about?'

What did I do?

'I don't want—' He swore and turned away, but then thought better of it and turned back. 'I don't want to hurt you, Tash.'

'Too late.' Her chest rose and fell several times as she gathered the courage to say what needed to be said. 'You gave me control, Aiden. You wanted me to take it.'

Ironic that she should be speaking of control while her voice was demonstrating so little of it.

'I told you, this isn't about tonight. Tonight was amazing.'

Pfft...words. He tried to touch her arm but she shook him off. 'Then what is it about?'

He curled his fingers back into his body. His blue eyes roiled with indecision. 'You're not someone I can see...fitting into my family.' He cleared his throat. 'Long term.'

Her stomach clenched hard and ice washed through her veins. It was only slightly better than what she'd feared. Both were rejections of who she essentially was. Humiliation surged up fast behind the ice. 'I must have missed your proposal.'

That did bring his eyes back to hers. 'A few weeks isn't going to change that. So why waste your time?'

Huh. If she'd imagined him overwhelmed with desire, she must have been projecting. Madly. 'Or yours?' she pressed.

He tipped the remnants of his mug into the sink and tightened his lips. 'This isn't about me.'

'No. It's about your family, apparently. But let's be honest. You mean your mother.'

'I have six aunts and uncles and their respective partners, too. None of them are going to accept the daughter of Adele Porter in their backyards, let alone their family.'

Tash's eyes strayed to where he'd been looking at the fridge. To the central display of a photo of her with her mother. And her heart ached.

'No. Not while no one challenges their prejudice.'

He hissed his frustration. 'You're expecting me to go up against my family for you.'

Yes, of course. How *inconceivable*. Clearly, she was nothing to him. 'Then why not do it for your father?'

His eyes narrowed. 'Leave my father out of this.'

'Poor Nathaniel must have been living in a war zone all these years. Enemy territory. With a bunch of hysterics who can't put the past in the past.' The steam was building pressure now. Every affront and resentment she'd ever felt at the hands of people who were blind and judgemental and stupid poured out onto her kitchen floor and onto his family. 'He abandoned the woman he loved to do the right thing by Laura and give you a father. And yes, he gave in to a momentary impulse when you and I were young but he stayed with Laura for *twenty years*, Aiden. To do the right thing by her again. But that's not enough for any of you, is it?'

He stood straighter and loomed a warning over her. 'Tash—'

'What the hell do you people want from us? I'm sorry he didn't love her more. But that's not my fault any more than my heritage is.'

'I could ask the same, Tash.' He breathed down on her hot and passionate. 'What the hell do you want from me? Give me some credit for trying to do the right thing by *you*, here. It would be so easy for me to just carry on with you, hiding the truth and having a good time for the weeks it would take me to bore of you.'

Was it so inevitable?

'You're every bit the cracker Jardine claimed. Why wouldn't I just take what you were so eagerly offering and enjoy it?' She winced but it didn't slow him any. 'But I'm not; I'm being chivalrous—and, believe me, gallantry is not my natural habitat—and ending it now before it goes any further with a woman who can have no place in my future.'

His words ricocheted off the shiny surfaces in the kitchen, making them endure painfully longer than the original. Once they subsided, the only sound was the respective heaving of their chests and lungs. In Tash's case, muted by the tight wadding of agony that pressed in around her thoracic cavity like saturated gauze around an open wound. She reached for the starfish she'd made with him the day before and clutched it to her heart for courage.

Would it be this way for ever, for her? *Tash Sinclair—for a good time but not a long time.*

'You're right,' she squeezed out past the bracing hurt, rich with sarcasm. 'Thank you for putting me out of my misery.' Unspent tears clogged her throat but she was damned if she'd let him see how much he'd hurt her. She ran her hands repeatedly over the cool, smooth glass of the sea star. 'It's ironic, really, that for you to be a man worthy of me you *have* to walk out that door.' She shuddered in a breath. 'And if you stayed then I'd be settling.'

His eyelids fell shut again.

'I don't know why I expected more. Everyone warned me that I shouldn't trust you, your father included. Turns out you're no different from the Kyle Jardines or the Eric Sinclairs.'

It wasn't until the words were out that Tash realised she never planned on calling him her father again.

Aiden's lashes lifted to reveal blazing anger.

'He beat his wife and six-year-old child for having the strength and character he lacked. It must have killed him to have that deficiency reflected a dozen times a day. Kyle, as well. Too emotionally insecure to maintain a proper relationship. I was stupid to think that you would be different. You're just as emotionally stunted as they are. You just dress better.'

His nostrils flared. 'Careful, Tash…'

'Or what, Aiden?' She pushed the challenge past the fist lodged in her throat. 'Do you imagine that you can do anything to me that my father didn't? Or say anything to me that Kyle didn't? I am over feeling diminished at the hands of men. If you're not into me enough to throw a single pebble into the dysfunctional surface of your family pond then that's fine, but at least *own it*. Don't preach to me about what a great man you're being by saving me the discomfort of not being welcome in your home. Your family would be *lucky* to have me in it. Maybe I'd add some character and strength to your diminishing gene pool.'

The insult hung, potent and awful, between them.

'It wouldn't be a pebble, Tash. I would be lobbing a grenade.'

She turned and threw the sea star against her hallway wall. It exploded into a hundred orange glassy fragments. 'Then hurl it, Aiden! Like the man I believed I'd fallen in love with. A strong and exciting and worthy man. God, I am so tired of *boys*.'

His body sagged and his voice, when it came, was tortured. 'You don't love me.'

She straightened, her chest racked with tight agony. 'Please don't measure me by your own standards. And please see yourself out.'

She turned and walked as steady as her wobbly legs would take her, over the broken glass and back into the bedroom where he'd conveniently removed all evidence of his presence while she slept off the after-effects of their passionate hours together.

She closed the door behind her and leaned on it, resolutely forbidding her eyes from filling, breath suspended and ears acutely honed to the noises coming from the other side of the door until her lungs burned with the need for air. The sounds of Aiden rinsing his mug and placing it on her stainless-steel draining board. Unlocking the internal deadlocks. Closing the door quietly behind him.

She welcomed the numbness, her old friend, and knew it would get her by until she could deal with the complicated mess of emotions burbling up inside her. It was only after she was certain that she had the acoustic protection of several walls between them that she let herself suck in a long-overdue breath and then slid down the door onto the carpet. She pushed her hair away from her face and stared in total confusion as her hands came away wet.

The tears she hadn't wanted to shed. The tears she hadn't even felt sliding down her face. Just like the lacerations on her bare feet that leaked a rich, awful crimson onto her mother's carpet.

The tears and blood—like the heartbreak—that spilled freely in total defiance to her will.

CHAPTER TWELVE

Six weeks later

IF NATHANIEL NOTICED they'd reverted to clandestine, just-the-two-of-them meetings to catch up, he didn't let on to Tash. His conversation, as it always was, was easy and low pressure, and she got the sense that he enjoyed the freedom of agenda-free exchanges as much as she did. He'd mentioned Aiden only twice. The first time her wince couldn't have failed to get his attention and, the second time, his scrutiny was so intense as he casually dropped his son's name into the discussion Tash knew he must have been fishing.

But when she'd kept her face rigid and let the clang of the name-drop go unanswered, he'd sat back and then carefully not mentioned Aiden again.

For weeks.

'So how's the new place working out?' she asked, stirring her latte.

'It's fine. I never was much of an accumulator; most of what I took with me we could stack on this café table so the size is fine.'

'Do you need anything?'

His hand curled around hers. 'Bless you, Tash. No. Anything I need I can buy.'

Oh, that's right. Money. She shrugged. 'Do you need company, then?'

Tiny lines forked at the corner of his eyes. 'Are you offering?'

'You know I enjoy our time together.' Lord. Was she actually as desperate as she sounded?

'Shouldn't you spend that time with your friends?'

'I thought *we* were friends.'

The look he gave her was so…fatherly. 'I'd love to see you any time.'

'At least I'll know you're not burying yourself in your work.'

'It's tempting, but no,' he said. 'One workaholic in the family is sufficient.'

Tash's entire body tightened. 'Is Aiden pulling long hours?' she asked as casually as she could. Like the carefully orchestrated mentions in her mother's diary. She had to start doing it some time.

Nathaniel snorted. 'Long, intense. And dragging others with him. He's presently the menace of the entire firm.' He studied her closely. 'Would you know anything about that?'

She was as bad with feigning innocence as she was with lying. 'When did it start?' she hedged.

'The day he found out my history with your mother.'

Her chest tightened. 'Well, there you go, then.'

'I assumed it was that but when I tried to speak to him about it he brushed me off as though he had more important things to think about.'

Maybe it was a guilty conscience. Good. She hoped that her parting words might have had some impact. She shrugged. 'Who knows?'

'Actually, I thought you might know, given the changes in your behaviour started right at the same time.'

Her eyes shot up to his. 'What changes?'

'You're so flat now. All the vibrancy and the joy you had are absent.'

It was true. She could see it in her work.

Nathaniel carefully picked his way through a bundle of things he obviously wanted to say. 'Tash, I don't care whether we're blood relatives or not—you have become as close to me as a daughter and I want to keep it that way. I'm worried about you.'

Strange that the question of her parentage was no longer even on her radar. Nor, truth be told, Eric Sinclair's absence in her life. Something about her miserable encounter with Aiden a few weeks back had given her some much-needed perspective.

People treated you exactly as you let them.

Had it really taken her thirty years to work that out?

She'd accused Aiden's family of living in the past, but wasn't that exactly what she was doing with her father? She was who she was; the why of it really didn't matter anymore. She would only drive herself crazy worrying about things she just couldn't change.

She smiled up at Nathaniel. 'I'd be happy to be your honorary daughter. Except—'

'Aiden is a grown man.' Nathaniel guessed the direction of her thoughts. 'He doesn't have to like our friendship but he has to accept it.'

'He's very complicated,' she whispered. 'And very conflicted.'

'I could have left Laura,' Nathaniel sighed, on a tangent. 'When you were young. It would have been the right time. But I saw the huge influence she was already having on Aiden and I knew that would go unchecked if I wasn't there to balance it out.'

Air rushed into Tash's lungs. 'You stayed for Aiden's sake?'

'I am not perfect, but I could at least remediate the worst

of Laura's own issues. Ensure he grew up a good man. A sane man.'

'You did well,' Tash breathed. *You know, except for the whole arrogant, narcissistic, emotional-cripple thing.*

'I often wished I had even part of your mother's fortitude. When the time came to do the tough thing, she just did it. She didn't look back. Perhaps Aiden would have been less affected if he'd been raised away from his parents' issues.'

She leaned over and slid her fingers onto his. 'You might not have had much of a relationship with him at all, then. And imagine what that would be like.'

She didn't have to imagine it. For her it was a reality.

Nathaniel separated his fingers so hers could slip between them. Then he squeezed. 'Whenever I got in a bind I used to think, *What would Adele do?*'

It was so close to what she did, herself, it was hard not to smile. 'What do you think she would have done differently in our position?'

He stared at her a moment, thinking. 'She would have done exactly what she always did. *Act.* Concrete positive action to change her situation. Not just waited to see what others would do.'

For weeks, the only path Tash could see ahead of her was dark, musty and singular. Forging onwards, forcing herself to forget Aiden and patching up her life as best she could. Surviving.

But Nathaniel's words blew a hole in the side of that tunnel, revealing a whole other pathway running parallel. Bright and filled with fresh air and the smell of violets. Like her mother's moisturiser. Forking off to the left.

Lord knew she was ready for a fork in her life. A new direction. A new way of doing things. Because the old way sure wasn't working. Maybe it was time to do more than just survive.

She sat up straighter at the café table.

Maybe it was time to fight.

She pulled their joined hands up to her lips. 'Nathaniel,' she whispered as he blushed. 'Has anyone ever told you that you are a brilliant man?'

'Someone once did.' His eyes twinkled dangerously with emotion. 'I'm so very glad I'm finally able to repay the compliment.'

The dying strains of Big Ben's chimes echoed in what was obviously an expansive hallway beyond the ornate front door. Tash ran her fingers along the shapes carved into its timber and waited for a response. The distinctive *click-clack* of approaching heels on marble came just a moment later, but they stopped at the front door and then…nothing. She could practically feel the gaze burning down onto her through the security peephole and the weight of the silence afterwards.

Would Laura open the door when she saw who'd rung the bell?

Seconds ticked by.

Maybe not.

'I just need a few moments of your time, Mrs Moore,' she offered in an even voice, eyes neutrally forward. Non-threatening. Like approaching a stressed-out dog.

Still nothing. Then, finally, the reluctant click of a deadlock and the door swung inward. Though not wide open, Tash noticed.

'Mrs Moore, I'm—'

'I know who you are,' Laura Moore began. 'What do you want?'

The words should have been rude, if they weren't so terribly defensive. And old. It struck her then how much beyond her actual age Laura Moore seemed. She must have turned fifty this year, too. But she seemed two decades older.

'I was hoping I could have a word with you.'

'About?'

Here went nothing... 'About your son. Please.'

That was the last thing Laura was expecting, obviously. Surprise had her stepping back, leaving a Tash-width aperture in the expensive doorway. She squeezed through into the ornate foyer and followed Laura into the house. Beyond the foyer, a luxurious home unfolded. Above them, at the top of a wide staircase, yet more rooms and landings sprawled. Tash's entire cottage could have fitted in Laura Moore's enormous kitchen, alone.

The phone rang and Laura excused herself to get it, murmured quietly and briefly into the handset, and then turned back to Tash, sliding it back into its cradle. 'What can I do for you, Miss Porter?'

'Sinclair.'

She didn't acknowledge the correction. 'I never expected to see you here.'

'No. I can imagine.' Tash glanced at four tall, leather stools peeking out from below the marble overhang of the expensive kitchen counters. 'Shall we sit?'

Laura didn't move. 'Will it take that long?'

Okay, defensive and now officially rude. 'I guess not.' She shifted her feet wider. 'I wanted to ask you about those days at uni with my mother and Nathaniel.'

She stiffened horribly. 'I thought you wanted to talk about Aiden.'

She stuck to her guns. 'It's related. Are you aware he now knows that Nathaniel and my mother were together before he married you?'

Judging by the way her colour bleached just slightly, no, she didn't.

'Aiden wouldn't have said anything to hurt me. He's very kind in that way.'

Kind or maybe just well trained in issues-avoidance.

Laura's lips pressed into a straight, rucked line. 'I assume I have you to thank for that?'

'Indirectly.' She took a deep breath. 'I thought I might have been Nathaniel's biological daughter.'

Two things happened then; the bleaching intensified and the most curious glint hardened in Laura's eyes. Like vindication. But it was wholly internal. Her voice, when it came, actually trembled. 'And…are you?'

'I am not.'

'Ah.'

That was a curious response. 'Did you expect me to be?'

Laura considered that for moments. 'It would have explained so much.'

'That's what I thought.'

'So you are Eric's?'

That threw her. 'As far as I'm aware.' Though she'd still give anything not to be, just on genetic grounds alone.

'Did that please you?'

Tash worked hard to keep the sarcasm out of her voice. Things were tense enough between them. 'No. Not at all.'

Laura nodded. 'I can imagine. Eric was a difficult young man. I can't imagine he improved with age.'

Out of nowhere, a new question burned on her tongue. 'Why were you friends with him?'

It seemed to throw Laura, too. But she shifted sideways and leaned against her expensive kitchen counter. 'Eric was just always…there. We formed a little group on orientation day and never really parted until—' she stumbled and changed tack '—until I withdrew from my studies. He was peripheral to the three of us and never seemed to understand that.'

Or maybe he had…only too well.

'You didn't like him?'

'I didn't trust him, particularly. None of us did.'

Rightly, as it turned out. But the opening was too good to pass up. 'Why would my mother marry him?'

Maybe it was the parent in Laura—unable to let another woman's child go unanswered on something so fundamental. Or maybe she'd just been telling herself this for so long. Consternation flitted across her face before she responded, 'Because he asked. And because she wanted to make a statement.'

It would be easy to imagine the latter, but not the former. 'I can't believe she would marry someone like that just because he asked.'

Laura's face pinched. 'She was…adrift. And he was available and eager. Your mother didn't like to be out of the centre of things.'

Tash bit her tongue. She had a purpose coming here today, and proving Aiden right by riling up his mother was not it. Besides, once again, Laura's words were laced with bitterness, not vindictiveness.

'Do you know why he was like that? Eric Sinclair?'

For the first time, Laura's eyes seemed to soften. 'He came from a broken family. Not very nice, if I remember rightly.'

Tash came from a not very nice broken situation, too, but she hoped she was nothing like him.

'And he loved your mother completely. He always did like shiny things.'

'He can't have loved her. Look how he treated her.' She wondered how much Laura knew about the punishment meted out to her mother before she found the strength to leave him.

'You weren't there, Natasha. You never saw how much he adored her, hovering like a bee to her daisy. But she never gave him the time of day.' That hard glint returned. 'Not until…'

'Until Nathaniel left her.' *For you.* 'So he should have

been the happiest man on the planet. Shouldn't he?' Something was off here.

'Can you imagine what it's like—' Laura gritted out '—to be the second choice of the person you love? That wouldn't have sat well with a fragile ego like Eric's. Even if he was getting what he wanted.'

Or with a damaged woman like Laura, Tash suddenly realised. How had she missed the obvious parallels in the two old friends?

'To have reminders thrust in your face every day,' Laura went on, warming up to her topic. 'Even in the things they didn't say. To have your own child named for another man.'

An ice covering formed on the confusion pooling in her gut. 'I'm named for Nathaniel?'

Those blue eyes, so like Aiden's yet so very different, hardened impossibly further. 'He always believed so.'

He who? Eric? Or Nathaniel?

She tried to imagine life with Aiden while he was secretly in love with someone else. And then she tried to imagine it wasn't a secret. How that would eat at you over time. The sudden realisation didn't make her like her father any better, but it did help explain his great slide into antipathy. 'But Mum was always very careful not to rub it in his face,' Tash defended. 'She didn't even use his name in her diaries.'

'Infinitely worse!' Laura barked. 'As though his name was something to be cherished and kept close. Or as if that made it even the slightest bit possible to forget what had gone before.'

Oh, they were definitely talking in code here. She absorbed Laura's words. 'Yes. I can see that. It must have been difficult.'

'Don't patronise me. Or him. Until you've lived it you can't understand.'

She stared at the older woman, her face wrought with a

lifetime of sorrow, and whispered, 'You still love Nathaniel, though. Even now?'

Fierceness filled her eyes. 'I will die loving that man.'

Just like her mother. 'Which is why you don't like me.'

'I don't have an opinion either way about you,' Laura spat her lie. 'Your mother and her offspring are of no consequence to me.'

Tash leaned in. 'You were friends,' she urged and Laura's face pinched. 'Her diaries are full of the great times you had together before it all went wrong. What happened?'

'My father happened,' a deep voice said from behind her. 'Isn't it always a man at the root of every female complaint?'

'Darling…' Laura's face and entire demeanour changed on seeing her son. Even her body language somehow grew more…frail. More vulnerable.

Viper.

'What are you doing here?' Laura purred.

Aiden threw her a frustrated, blank look. 'You pressed the panic alarm. We spoke by phone a few minutes ago. I came because I thought it was an emergency.' He turned his glare onto Tash, punishing her for wasting his time. As if *she'd* pressed some duress button. 'Instead I find the two of you in a cosy tête-à-tête.'

A thousand miles from cosy. Tash squared her shoulders against the hot surge that seeing him birthed, and faced his scorn. 'I decided that if your family's inability to accept me was all that was stopping us being together then I'd see if there wasn't something I could do about that.'

Behind her, Laura gasped.

Aiden's brows dipped. 'Proactive, as always—'

For Aiden, that was a very mild response. Would she get off that lightly?

'—and deluded, as always.'

Right. *Good to see you, too.*

'You got here very quickly,' Tash commented, all suspicion.

'It's Saturday. I was working at home.'

A silver thread stretched out between them, binding them together. 'Your father said you were pulling long hours,' she whispered.

'Aiden lives in the next street,' Laura announced apropos of nothing. 'Family's always been important to him.' It was a gush but it wasn't for her benefit. In fact, it reeked of a reminder. Or maybe an instruction.

Aiden looked as if he found it about as distasteful as Tash did.

'Tea, darling?' Laura cooed to Aiden. 'Natasha, are you sure I can't persuade you?'

Oh, please. But growing up the daughter of Eric Sinclair had at least taught her what to do with passive aggression. Play the game.

'Well, perhaps if it's a party…' She threw out a tight smile.

'Don't let me interrupt your conversation,' Aiden challenged, locking eyes with hers. They said, *What the hell are you doing here?*

Tash swallowed the ache and lifted her chin. *I'm fighting for what I want.* 'How much did you hear?'

'You were asking about your mother and mine, what happened to their friendship.'

Not an answer. Which meant he could have heard everything, or nothing.

Laura waved an elegantly manicured but papery hand. It reminded Tash, suddenly, of something that might flop out of a sarcophagus. She placed the kettle back onto its electric base and set it to boil. 'Oh, you know how it is. Those years of your life are so dynamic. Friendships come and go.'

'Mother's first diary is full of her sadness as your friendship waned.' If she wanted to do this in front of a witness, fine.

Laura turned bitter eyes in her direction, not quite as gracious or befuddled as she'd gifted Aiden with. She thought it was secret, but Tash saw Aiden see it in the mirrored splashback behind the induction cooktop. 'Adele always was good at turning it on and off as required.'

'Was it only about Nathaniel? The troubles between you?'

'My goodness, you certainly inherited her sense of entitlement!' Laura blustered, all wit and sarcasm. 'As if someone as *delightful* and *fabulous* as Adele should automatically be loved by all.' She slapped her hands on the counter. 'She was as flawed as the next person. She and Eric deserved each other in my opinion.'

'Mum…' Aiden murmured, dangerous and low.

Nausea threatened deep in Tash's throat. 'Really? She deserved overnights in hospital and being beaten with a phonebook so the bruises would be less distinct? She deserved the coroner's investigation when she died because of the number of old injuries on her body?'

Laura's hands froze in the midst of dropping a gourmet teabag into each of three designer cups. But she pulled herself together enough to finish the job. But not enough to stop her hands from trembling visibly. She tucked them out of view as soon as she could and turned to pour the kettle. She lifted it as though it weighed a ton and then replaced it succinctly onto its base when her unsteady hands couldn't keep it still.

Finally, she half turned back to Tash and whispered, 'He beat her?'

Tash nodded and Laura echoed it, though slower and jerkier. Aiden crossed behind his mother and poured the cups for her, placing a supporting hand on her shoulder. That little bit of solidarity only undid her more. She slid her own up to thread through her son's fingers.

'I didn't know it was that bad,' she whispered, all pretence vanished.

Tash clenched her teeth. 'But you knew it was happening?'

'It was Eric.' She shuddered in a breath. 'I discovered Nathaniel's expenditure. The legal costs. That little house. I forced him to explain. But he never said why she had to get out, just that she had. I assumed…'

She couldn't finish and Tash knew what that meant. Laura had assumed it was a prelude to Nathaniel taking back up with Adele.

'He saved both our lives that day.'

Laura nodded. 'He would have done anything for her.'

'Mum—'

'No, Aiden. Enough.' She turned haunted eyes up to him. 'I'm so tired of all of this. Time that it all came out.'

'Without Dad here?'

'He knows all of it. He's always known.'

'Known what?'

She turned to Tash. 'Adele shouldn't have valued my advice, Natasha. It was selfish advice.'

'What do you mean?'

'She confided in me, about Nathaniel pressuring her to… consummate their relationship. And he confided in me as well, his fears that her not wanting to be intimate meant she didn't care for him the way he did for her.' Her laugh was dark. 'It was so easy to turn their minds. To convince *him* he was right and to convince *her* that holding out would be good for their relationship.'

'They trusted you.'

'Of course they did.'

'What are you saying, Mum?'

She spun on her son. 'I wanted them apart. I wanted an end to the endless soap opera that was Adele and Nathaniel's great love affair and I wanted to turn the friendship that I had with him into more.'

'You broke them up,' Tash whispered.

'Oh, don't say it as though I defaced some holy relic,' she hissed. 'I seized my chance. My future. I knew what I wanted and I went for it. I won't pity Adele for waiting for the world to give her things. She already had beauty and intelligence and—' She bit back the rest.

'And Nathaniel?'

'To the victor go the spoils. That's how it works. Well, I was the victor.'

'Until you weren't,' Tash whispered. 'He went back to her.'

'And then returned to me.'

Intense pity suffused Aiden's face. His hand squeezed on Laura's shoulder and his eyes fell shut.

'He just needed time. He just needed an opportunity to love me.'

Aiden turned her slowly and stared down on her. 'Was I that opportunity?'

Her whole body trembled now. 'He was a good man,' she urged up into Aiden's face. 'He just needed a good reason to come back to me. To get out from under her influence.'

And a pregnancy was a very good reason indeed.

'You trapped Nathaniel,' Tash whispered. And destroyed a whole bunch of lives in one fell swoop.

Aiden's hand slipped from her mother's shoulder and he turned and braced himself on the opposite counter.

'It wasn't a trap,' she urged. The earnest proclamation of the condemned. 'It was a *reason*.'

Tash stared; saw the fragile, broken women that must have lived under the gloss and glamour. Perpetually. Even back then.

'I've blamed him for so many years,' Aiden whispered. 'I was convinced he'd done you great wrong.'

'He did do me wrong,' she begged. 'He *slept* with her.'

'He was desperate,' Tash murmured. 'He discovered my father's brutality and he wanted to save her, but she wouldn't let him leave you. So he staged it so that Eric would find out.'

Laura spun on her, fire in her eyes below the tears. 'No. She would have taken him in a heartbeat.'

'It's true. It's in her diary and Nathaniel told me, too. She wanted him to go back to his family.'

Panic filled her face. 'No!'

'Why "no", Laura? Does it upset you to think maybe she was a good person after all? That the woman you cheated out of her love didn't deserve what you did to her? That you abandoned your friend and set her up to be with a man who abused her horribly?'

Her thin lips opened and closed wordlessly. She turned and begged Aiden with her panicked gaze. 'Why is she here?'

'I'm here because I want the truth.' Tash moved around to put herself directly in Laura's line of vision and she locked onto her eyes. 'I'm here because I know what I want and I'm going for it. *I'm* seizing my chance just like you did.'

'You want Aiden,' she nearly shrieked.

'I absolutely do.'

Behind her, Aiden straightened and then walked past them both, out of the kitchen and through a sliding door to the pool deck.

Laura turned on her with triumph. 'Looks like the feeling is not mutual.'

Every part of her tightened. 'That might be true, but I'm only going to accept that from him. Hasn't there been enough lies and deception in this family?'

'It's not bad enough that *she* got Nathaniel's heart, now I have to give you Aiden's?'

The sneer finally got to her. Tash struck back. 'Maybe the hearts of the Moore men have always belonged in my family? Maybe this is just the universe putting things to rights?'

'No!' Laura's wail was pain incarnate. And broken.

Pity swamped through Tash for a woman who was so crippled by fear that she'd let it run her whole life. 'I don't want it exclusively, Laura,' she urged. 'I could never love a man who didn't cherish his family.' She glanced up at where Aiden paced, furious, along the decking surrounding the opulent swimming pool and then back at his bitter, fearful mother. 'But I want my chance. And I'm taking it.'

Mascara-streaked eyes widened and stared, and then dropped to where her fingers twisted in front of her. 'You're just like her, you know,' she murmured, disarmed.

'Like Mum?'

'Adele had a very strong sense of what was right and wrong. I knew that. Despite everything.'

'You knew she wouldn't fight for Nathaniel.'

Breath wheezed out of her. 'I counted on it. I'm so sorry that you lost her so young. There but for the grace of God….'

Tash was nearly overcome by the strength of the hatred coursing through her. For what this weak woman had done to her mother's life. But she forced it to morph and change. Into pity. And acceptance. She'd meant it when she said she was tired of living in the past.

'Thank you.'

'We were true friends. At the start. I hope that Adele knew that.'

'She knew.'

And then no more words would come. Laura just nodded and turned back to finish making the tea that nobody wanted. Tash stepped back, turned her eyes to the pool deck and started walking. But as she reached the door a croaky voice reached her.

'I made him into the man he is, you know...' Tash stopped, looked back at Laura. Was she still going to stake her claim on her son? But a broken heart shone through in her red-rimmed eyes as she lifted them. 'This man that can't trust love.'

Tash nodded and looked around this beautiful, empty, soul-less home. 'Why would he?'

And then she pulled on the door.

'Aiden?'

He stopped where he stood, his back still to her. 'Did you suspect?'

'I had no idea. I just wanted to talk to her, try to understand where you're coming from. Try and change it.'

He nodded. 'Do you think Dad knows she got pregnant on purpose?'

'I think so. He always seemed on the verge of saying more. But he never did.'

'Still doing the right thing by her.'

Her chest lifted and then slowly deflated. 'Yeah.'

'Do you think there's any future for them?' he asked, monotone.

No. Not according to Nathaniel. 'Perhaps it's time he put himself first?'

Aiden turned, found her eyes. Found her soul. 'He's earned it.'

She stepped closer and curled a hand around his wrist.

'I've misjudged him so much,' he whispered.

'He understands.'

'You're very certain.'

'You're his son. The only person in his life that he's free to love unconditionally. He's not going to give up on that lightly.'

'He loves you, too.'

Tash smiled. 'For who I remind him of.'

'And for who you are. He told me.' Clouded eyes held hers.

'He's made discussing you in my presence a sport.' His eyes flicked to the house. 'When she told me on the phone you were here…I thought you'd come to force my hand.'

'You looked pretty mad when you walked in.'

'Your persistence riled me even as your courage shamed me.'

'No…'

'You confronted my family, knowing how they felt about yours. Knowing how she would be. Why did you do that?'

'Because all my life I've ceded power to other people. My father. Kyle. Even you to some extent. It was time I took control into my own hands.'

'By fronting the lion's den?'

'Wounded lions always lash out.'

'You don't judge her?'

'What she told us is going to take a lot of getting past. But she's lived with her own judgement all these years; I don't think mine would add much value.'

His eyes narrowed. 'That's very generous.'

'It's not generous, it's just smart.' At his blank look, she elaborated. 'If I want to be in your life.'

'Tash—'

'I know what you said. I just don't believe you. This can't be just about your family.'

'You believed it enough to come here.'

The tension in her shoulders made shrugging a strain. 'I'm covering all my bases.'

'And now?'

She took a deep breath. 'You were right when you said I could never fit comfortably in your family. I couldn't. But what you failed to understand is that I'm prepared to live uncomfortably in it. For you.'

His gaze intensified. His throat lurched. 'That's no way to live. Look at my father.'

'It wouldn't be my first preference.'

'I thought you were done ceding power to others?'

'Don't get me wrong. I'm not saying I wouldn't move heaven and earth to change it. I'm saying you're worth the discomfort.'

His eyes slated sideways. 'I thought I was no more *worthy* than I am strong or exciting. Or manly.'

'I'm not perfect either. I wanted you bleeding the way I was.'

'Oh, I've bled, Tash. You have no idea.'

'Why? If I meant so little to you.'

He paced to the corner of the pool, then retraced his steps. 'So much of who I am is based on who I thought he was,' Aiden muttered. 'I saw and heard more than everyone believed back then. I knew what he'd done. *Thought* I knew,' he corrected himself. 'And on some level I think I took my cues about relationships there. How vulnerable you are to hurt when you give yourself—your heart—to someone else.'

'It's not like that for everyone.'

'I wonder if your mother ever said that to my father?'

'And *I* wonder how much might have been different if they'd been honest with each other from the start. Not made all those assumptions.'

'Do you think it would have changed his decision when he found out Mum was pregnant?'

'No. Because he was and still is a man who owned his actions. But I don't think he would have gone with her in the first place.'

'Then you and I wouldn't exist. We never would have met.'

Was that what he wanted, deep down? Would it be easier, for both of them, if she'd never opened her mother's diaries? Never opened the door to her curiosity? Perhaps. But easier was not necessarily better.

She peered up at him. 'Meeting you was a turning point

for me. *Being* with you. I don't like how it came out but I wouldn't wish it undone for anything.'

A small bird flitted down into the garden and made a show of bouncing between perfectly manicured shrubs. Tash fixated on it.

Aiden cleared his throat. 'I need you to know something, Tash. I didn't know, going in, how I was going to feel on the other side of us sleeping together.'

At least he hadn't said *having* sex. But it was a long mile from *making love*, which was how she'd viewed it. When she wasn't thinking of it as *changing her forever.*

'I was numb coming out of the meeting with my father. The only thing that could pierce that was you. Your presence and your touch. I craved it.' His eyes dropped. 'I used it, to distract myself from the reality of everything I'd learned. I used you. And I hate that.'

'I'm not all that crazy about it, either,' she muttered.

'My experience of relationships has been limited,' he admitted.

She gaped. 'I read the newspapers, Aiden. I have an Internet connection.'

'I'm not talking about quantity. I'm talking about scope. I've had hundreds of the same kind of relationship. Fast, limited. Safe. I'm sure the papers don't cover that.' He plunged his hands into his pockets. 'You were a totally new experience for me. Someone who challenged me. Someone who bested me. Someone who was quite prepared to be disrespectful of me.'

He roamed back and forth across the deck. Tash stood frozen.

'And then we stood in your apartment on the verge of being together and I saw how nervous you were to really be free with me, and I burned with such intensity I was overwhelmed.'

Doubt washed through her. The old distrust. 'Out of your hundreds of experiences?'

'I'm not talking about my raging desire to *take* you. I'm talking about the force of my desire to take *care* of you. To protect you, even with me, and with anyone else you would ever meet. I wanted to liberate you from the doubt that jerk Jardine instilled in you and beat your stinking father to death with my bare hands for how he treated you. I woke up next to you and never, ever wanted to wake up next to anyone else. Ever. You were so brave and so wild and so perfect and that…terrified me.'

A thick clog of tears mustered high in her chest.

'And then you smashed the starfish—*my* starfish—and I realised that's what I'd done to you. Broken this fragile, beautiful thing into pieces. Maybe never to go back together. With my own cowardice.'

'You're not a coward, Aiden—'

'You called it, Tash. I wasn't prepared to go up against my family for you. My mother. Our whole life has been about maintaining the status quo, keeping her happy. She raised me to be the man she wanted my father to be. Compliant and loving and all-worshipping. In fact, she's pretty much conditioned the people around her to be like that too.'

'Aiden, don't—'

He shook his head. 'I would have happily beaten a man to death for you but I wouldn't risk bringing you home for dinner. What kind of a man does that?'

'An imperfect man. A human man.'

His snort turned ugly. 'A child.'

'You *were* a child when these patterns were set. As controlled by your mother as I was by my father.'

'She's so manipulative. I'm only just seeing it.'

'She's also your mother. You don't get two of those. And all of those things she did for you as a child are still valid.'

He turned his confusion up to her. 'You have more reason than anyone to hate what she's done.'

She tipped her face to the sky. 'Enough with the hate between our families. If I can accept it, then so can you. Her legacy nearly hurt us both but it didn't. We stopped it. We're both standing here. We can't change the past, only the present.' She moved directly in front of him. 'So, Aiden Moore, what are you going to do with the present? That's what counts.'

His nostrils flared wildly. 'I barely know what to do.'

'Me neither.'

'I have no right to expect anything from you. After what I did.'

'No. You can't expect. But you can hope. And you can ask.' She stepped up and circled her arms around his neck. 'And I can deliver.'

His hands curled around behind her as if they were independent of his body. 'You'd do that?'

'Yes, I would. In fact, I think it's time for a new commission for MooreCo.'

He tipped his head. 'You haven't finished the first one yet.'

'This one is going to be something special. Something with unlimited facets and so much glorious potential. My best work yet.'

'What is it?'

'I'm going to smelt us a life together. And you're going to help me. Sharpen my tools with your insight, fuel the furnace with your passion and keep me safe from the flames with your love. We'll display it in our first home together.'

He bent and pressed his lips to the soft place behind her ear. 'Love,' he murmured. 'Is that what this is? This total inability to sleep, this horrible, churning stomach when I think about that night? This feverish sweat when I remember our one night together?'

One night. That was all her mother ever had with Nathaniel. And, for the first time, she understood how one night might have fuelled a passion that lasted twenty more years.

She curled her arms even higher and breathed into his skin. 'Yeah, stupid. That's love.'

'I thought maybe I was getting your flu.'

'You look too good for someone with the flu.'

'You never know.'

'I should take your temperature.' And she did, with her lips, long, hard and hot. 'Wow, you are kind of warm,' she breathed. 'Maybe I should bring you soup.'

'Only if you have it with me. In bed.'

He kissed her again and her head swam with the closeness. It was so much more than proximity. This closeness went cell deep and bonded them on a level Tash had never imagined was possible. This closeness was the same she got in her hot shop, melding two pieces of glass together with a blowtorch. You never melded two of the same pieces of glass because then you just had glass. But bond two very different pieces together and you had something new. Something surprising and risky and beautiful.

You had a work of art.

'If this is love,' Aiden whispered into her lips, 'I don't ever want to get better.'

'Your mother?' Tash gasped as she surfaced for air.

'She'll have to learn to live with it.'

Light surged through her body and it carried the same gooseflesh, the same tingling rightness that she'd once associated with endorsement from her mother's spirit. 'And your father?' she asked, for Adele.

'I have a lot to make up to him for. But he'll want to give you away at our wedding. And then accept you into the Moore family.'

She pushed against that rock-hard, beautiful chest, mouth agape. 'We're having a wedding?'

'At some point. Not this week. I need to see how the original MooreCo piece works out. See if you're the right artist for our life together. You might not be.'

'Aiden Moore, you conceited—'

But that was as far as she got because those beautiful, conceited lips stole her words—and her breath—completely away.

* * * * *

ROMANCE

His Most Exquisite Conquest	Emma Darcy
One Night Heir	Lucy Monroe
His Brand of Passion	Kate Hewitt
The Return of Her Past	Lindsay Armstrong
The Couple who Fooled the World	Maisey Yates
Proof of Their Sin	Dani Collins
In Petrakis's Power	Maggie Cox
A Shadow of Guilt	Abby Green
Once is Never Enough	Mira Lyn Kelly
The Unexpected Wedding Guest	Aimee Carson
A Cowboy To Come Home To	Donna Alward
How to Melt a Frozen Heart	Cara Colter
The Cattleman's Ready-Made Family	Michelle Douglas
Rancher to the Rescue	Jennifer Faye
What the Paparazzi Didn't See	Nicola Marsh
My Boyfriend and Other Enemies	Nikki Logan
The Gift of a Child	Sue MacKay
How to Resist a Heartbreaker	Louisa George

MEDICAL

Dr Dark and Far-Too Delicious	Carol Marinelli
Secrets of a Career Girl	Carol Marinelli
A Date with the Ice Princess	Kate Hardy
The Rebel Who Loved Her	Jennifer Taylor

Mills & Boon® Large Print

July 2013

ROMANCE

Playing the Dutiful Wife	Carol Marinelli
The Fallen Greek Bride	Jane Porter
A Scandal, a Secret, a Baby	Sharon Kendrick
The Notorious Gabriel Diaz	Cathy Williams
A Reputation For Revenge	Jennie Lucas
Captive in the Spotlight	Annie West
Taming the Last Acosta	Susan Stephens
Guardian to the Heiress	Margaret Way
Little Cowgirl on His Doorstep	Donna Alward
Mission: Soldier to Daddy	Soraya Lane
Winning Back His Wife	Melissa McClone

HISTORICAL

The Accidental Prince	Michelle Willingham
The Rake to Ruin Her	Julia Justiss
The Outrageous Belle Marchmain	Lucy Ashford
Taken by the Border Rebel	Blythe Gifford
Unmasking Miss Lacey	Isabelle Goddard

MEDICAL

The Surgeon's Doorstep Baby	Marion Lennox
Dare She Dream of Forever?	Lucy Clark
Craving Her Soldier's Touch	Wendy S. Marcus
Secrets of a Shy Socialite	Wendy S. Marcus
Breaking the Playboy's Rules	Emily Forbes
Hot-Shot Doc Comes to Town	Susan Carlisle

0613 GEN STD LP

ROMANCE

The Billionaire's Trophy	Lynne Graham
Prince of Secrets	Lucy Monroe
A Royal Without Rules	Caitlin Crews
A Deal with Di Capua	Cathy Williams
Imprisoned by a Vow	Annie West
Duty At What Cost?	Michelle Conder
The Rings that Bind	Michelle Smart
An Inheritance of Shame	Kate Hewitt
Faking It to Making It	Ally Blake
Girl Least Likely to Marry	Amy Andrews
The Cowboy She Couldn't Forget	Patricia Thayer
A Marriage Made in Italy	Rebecca Winters
Miracle in Bellaroo Creek	Barbara Hannay
The Courage To Say Yes	Barbara Wallace
All Bets Are On	Charlotte Phillips
Last-Minute Bridesmaid	Nina Harrington
Daring to Date Dr Celebrity	Emily Forbes
Resisting the New Doc In Town	Lucy Clark

MEDICAL

Miracle on Kaimotu Island	Marion Lennox
Always the Hero	Alison Roberts
The Maverick Doctor and Miss Prim	Scarlet Wilson
About That Night...	Scarlet Wilson

Mills & Boon® Large Print
August 2013

ROMANCE

Master of her Virtue	Miranda Lee
The Cost of her Innocence	Jacqueline Baird
A Taste of the Forbidden	Carole Mortimer
Count Valieri's Prisoner	Sara Craven
The Merciless Travis Wilde	Sandra Marton
A Game with One Winner	Lynn Raye Harris
Heir to a Desert Legacy	Maisey Yates
Sparks Fly with the Billionaire	Marion Lennox
A Daddy for Her Sons	Raye Morgan
Along Came Twins…	Rebecca Winters
An Accidental Family	Ami Weaver

HISTORICAL

The Dissolute Duke	Sophia James
His Unusual Governess	Anne Herries
An Ideal Husband?	Michelle Styles
At the Highlander's Mercy	Terri Brisbin
The Rake to Redeem Her	Julia Justiss

MEDICAL

The Brooding Doc's Redemption	Kate Hardy
An Inescapable Temptation	Scarlet Wilson
Revealing The Real Dr Robinson	Dianne Drake
The Rebel and Miss Jones	Annie Claydon
The Son that Changed his Life	Jennifer Taylor
Swallowbrook's Wedding of the Year	Abigail Gordon

0713 GEN STD LP